When you make your living robbing criminals, you never know when your time is going to run out.

After the Travelers cheated the Orange Hill Cartel, the cartel sent a team of contract killers to hunt them down. Now every job the Travelers try, the killers close in, disrupting the scam just as the Travelers are about to cash out.

So the Travelers have gone to ground in the Colorado mountains, hiding in a cabin up a dirt road. After they run out of money, they take a short-term job robbing an embezzling banker in Rocky Shore, Missouri, hoping to get in and out before the killers can find them.

But when the killers crash this job, the Travelers barely escape after a shootout on the city streets. Can they stay one step ahead of the killers long enough to hatch a plan to deal with them and get the Orange Hill Cartel off their backs for good?

The Contract Killers is a cat-and-mouse cross-country race against time. If you like unpredictable plot twists, criminal shenanigans, and nail-biting suspense, you'll love the eleventh novel in the Travelers series.

I0618990

THE CONTRACT KILLERS

THE TRAVELERS
BOOK 11

MICHAEL P KING

Blurred Lines Press

The Contract Killers

Michael P. King

ISBN 978-1-952711-19-0

Cover design by Paramita Bhattacharjee at creativeparamita.com

For Sarah

1

"Criminals we've robbed wanting us dead is a given. Having to run so fast that there's no time to enjoy the money we're stealing, that's the problem." Allen put his coffee cup down on the counter.

The Travelers, now going by the names Allen and Janet Moore, stood at the kitchen counter in a two-room cabin down a dirt road in Roosevelt National Forest in Colorado, drinking coffee after breakfast. Allen was an anonymous-looking, middle-age man about six feet tall. He didn't look like an athlete, but he was hard and quick when he couldn't talk his way out of a bad situation. Janet, several years younger, looked like a Disney princess on the cusp of middle age with her perfect skin, dancer's curves, and hair pulled back in a ponytail. She could charm men or women out of their clothes or secrets with a smile and a touch.

"Honey, I agree," Janet replied. "Having to hide is a bummer, but we've got more immediate problems. We're almost out of money."

"What do you expect? Sean and Phyllis crashed our last two jobs. We almost didn't outrun them in Cleveland. They've got some way of figuring out where we're at."

"So we've got to move faster and disappear sooner."

"This life used to be a lot more fun."

"It always is when people aren't trying to murder us. Maybe it's time to retire," she said.

"On what? We don't have that kind of money. Not even if we pull together the work stashes we've got spread out in banks all over the country. You going to get a straight job? Doing what? You've got no work history."

"So short term we need walking around money and long term we need a retirement account."

"We've got to get the Orange Hill Cartel off our backs so we can go back to earning."

"We don't want to mess with them anymore," Janet said. "That'll just bring more heat."

"As if Sean and Phyllis aren't enough?"

"They're just one contract team. You think Orange Hill won't put another one on us if Sean and Phyllis can't get the job done? I think we have to expect the unexpected." Janet put her empty coffee cup in the sink. "Baby, I love you, but we've been over this again and again. This conversation is not going anywhere. I'm going to the Safeway for groceries. You want anything?"

"Can you stop by the liquor store? We're about out of bourbon."

After Janet drove off down the windy road through the thick woods, Allen poured another cup of coffee and sat out on the porch, his AR-15 rifle leaning against the wall beside him.

The air smelled of pine, birds flitted through the branches, and if he listened as hard as he could, he could hear the stream running though the rapids in the valley to the west. What to do about their situation? The pressure was on. After the job blackmailing that prosecuting attorney in Ohio turned to mud, they'd had to dip back into an old job in Chicago to make their escape. But that was one score too many for the Orange Hill Cartel. They hired contract killers to track them down, and they'd been dodging them ever since. He and Janet had to find a way to get them off their backs so that they could successfully disappear and go back to their normal lives.

Allen's burner phone rang. He looked at the number on the screen. Billy. Their go-to guy for jobs and equipment. "Yeah?"

"You still looking for work?"

"It's got to be quick and easy."

"I've got you a banker who's embezzling from trust accounts. It's a slow drip, mixed in the beneficiaries' requests for funds."

"How do you know?"

"A bank examiner has been getting a taste. But now he wants more. He'll put you into the game for $10,000."

"That's a pretty high finder's fee."

"There's supposed to be a lot of money involved. The banker has been stashing the money in a private account. Get the account codes. Move the cash. Might take you a couple of weeks of set-up. You're in, you're out."

"You certain it's worth the trouble?"

"You know what I know."

"I'll call you back." He ended the call.

After Janet returned from the grocery store, Allen helped her carry in the groceries and then filled her in on his conversation with Billy. "If the job is even half of what it's claimed to be, this is easy money. What do you think?"

Janet turned from the open refrigerator. "It's not going to be as easy as they say."

"Never is."

"But we've got to work. We're going to run out of ready cash sitting here. I say it's worth the risk."

"Okay." He called Billy. "We're in. Just to be clear, it's $10,000 up front and then your twelve percent of the score after we deduct the $10,000."

"I can do that."

"What's the bank examiner's name?"

"Carl Thompson."

"Have him call us tomorrow at 9:00 a.m. our time to fill in the details." He gave Billy the phone number of an unused burner phone.

"Will do."

That afternoon, Janet did an internet search on Carl Thompson. He was stationed out of the St. Louis Federal Reserve. Married. One kid in elementary school, one kid in high school. His wife was a dental assistant. Just a happy, middle-class family.

"Just a normal Joe with his hand in the till," Janet said.

"No gambling? No girlfriend? No extravagance?"

She shook her head. "Nothing hinting at a hidden life."

"Wonder where his wife thinks the money comes from?"

"Maybe she knows. Maybe he's slipping it into an IRA."

"So we're taking the call?"

"Let's hear him out."

THE NEXT MORNING at 9:00, Allen got a phone call on the burner phone. He called Janet over to the kitchen table and put the phone on speaker.

"Hello?" the voice said.

"You know a friend of ours?" Allen asked.

"Billy? Yeah."

"You're Carl Thompson?"

"Yeah."

"Okay. Give us the overview."

"Benny Singh, a banker at Freedom Bank and Trust in Rocky Shore, Missouri, is pulling money from trust accounts and funneling it into his personal mutual fund account. There're some steps in between, but that's the gist."

"And you know this how?"

"I examined the bank's books and found the discrepancies in the trust accounts."

"So you've been getting paid?"

"And I'll continue to get paid. The $10,000 is a bonus I'm giving myself."

"And you know for a fact that the cash is in the mutual fund account?"

"At least a couple hundred thousand."

"What can you tell us about Singh?"

"Divorced. Big spender. Thinks he's a lady's man. His personal assistant pays his bills."

"So you think that's the way in?"

"I don't know. That's your area of expertise."

Allen glanced at Janet. She nodded.

"Okay, we'll do the job," he said. "How do you want to receive payment?"

"Bank transfer."

"What're the routing number and account number?"

He gave them the information.

"You'll receive your money after the job is done."

"I want my money now."

"Yeah, but you can't rat us out until you've got your money, so you'll wait."

"You've got a bleak view of the world. What makes you think I'm that kind of guy?"

"'Cause that's what you're doing to your current partners. Don't call again." Allen ended the call. "Almost sounds too easy."

Janet nodded. "We need access to Singh's computer and the password to his mutual fund account, but once we have them, we should be in business."

Janet opened her laptop, went onto the internet, and did a deep dive into Benny Singh's life. He was divorced, but there was no information about his ex-wife or children on the internet or social media. He lived in a condo in downtown Rocky Shore. He'd been the Vice President for Trusts at Freedom Bank and Trust for eight years. He'd been divorced five years. Jay Cohen was his personal assistant, and Olivia Blevins was his second in command. He and Olivia also owned Elemental Security, which specialized in background investigations and bounty hunting.

"Looks like Singh and Blevins have a side hustle doing investigations and money recovery for the bank," she said.

Allen looked at the screen over her shoulder. "Nice little bit of nepotism. Wonder what they kick back to the bank's president."

"Makes me wonder if the whole bank is crooked," she replied.

"Let's not get ahead of ourselves. Running a score against the bank could take six months. Let's stick with the job we know."

"Okay, just let me dig into Cohen and Blevins a bit."

Two DAYS LATER, Allen and Janet drove into Rocky Shore, Missouri, a tourist community on the Mississippi river south of St. Louis. The downtown was mainly boutique shops and restaurants. Pleasure boats were moored along the wharf near the paddle-wheeler dock.

"You've got to love a tourist town," Allen said. "No one's going to notice two new faces."

"We've made a lot of money in these kinds of towns."

"Yes, we have."

They found their Airbnb on a quiet street in a middle-class neighborhood. Three middle- school-age boys were riding bikes in the street and an older man was walking a German shepherd. They pulled into the driveway, rolled their bags into the front entryway, and carried groceries into the kitchen. "Okay," Allen said. "Tomorrow you need to rope in Singh's assistant."

"Shouldn't be a problem. He's single, straight, and his social media shows him on vacation with older women who don't look like aunts."

"Just our kind of guy."

THEN NEXT MORNING, Allen and Janet sat in a rented Nissan Sentra, watching the front of the downtown offices of the Freedom Bank and Trust. A little after 9:00 a.m., Jay Cohen, Singh's personal assistant, came out of the bank and walked down the sidewalk. Jay was a tall, thin man with a tightly trimmed beard. He wore a conservatively cut black suit and a striped tie. Janet, wearing a fluttery dress that was tight in all the right places, got out of the Sentra and followed him into a nearby Caffeination Coffee Shop, where she overheard his order and ordered the same drink. Then she followed him to the end of the counter. When his drink was called, she bumped into him just as he turned from the counter. His drink splattered on the floor.

"I'm so sorry," she said, touching his arm. "It's like I can't even see in the morning." Her drink was called. She immediately grabbed it and held it out to him. "Please. Take mine."

"I'll order a new one," he said.

"Don't be silly," she replied. "I owe you a drink. What was yours?"

"Cappuccino with whole milk."

"That's what this is."

"Really?"

"Really." She handed him the cappuccino. "I didn't get any on you, did I?"

"No, I'm fine."

"You sure?"

"Yes."

"I'll pay for the dry-cleaning."

"No worries."

An employee came out of the back room and guided a bucket of soapy water with a string mop through the people waiting in the line. "I've got to go," Cohen said. He pushed through the front doors of the coffee shop.

Janet stood in the window and watched until she saw him go back into the bank. Then she hurried back down the street to the Sentra.

"Well?"

"A few more run-ins and he'll be eating out of my hand."

At 12:30 p.m., Cohen came out of the bank and walked up the street to the Blue Parrot Deli. Janet followed a few minutes later. The place was jammed. All the stools at the counter were full and all the tables were occupied. Janet saw Cohen sitting by himself, reading a menu. She walked over to his table. "Excuse me," she said. "Can I join you?"

Cohen looked up from his menu and did a double take. "Wait a second. You're the lady with the coffee this morning."

She smiled. "Guilty."

He gestured toward the opposite chair.

"Thank you." She sat down. "I'm Janet, by the way."

"I'm Jay. You come here often?"

"First time."

"Really? Do you work downtown?"

"No, I'm retired. Just looking for a change of scenery."

"Must be nice."

"Being retired? It is."

"Need to look at the menu?"

"Thanks."

Their server came. Cohen ordered a Rueben and an iced tea. Janet ordered the mixed green salad with salmon and a glass of white wine.

"So, Jay, you must work downtown."

"At Freedom Bank."

"Like it?"

"Well," he said, "I'm a personal assistant, so my boss's mood can have a lot to do with how my day goes."

She smiled and reached across to touch his hand. "Let's hope he —or she—is always in a good mood."

"It can vary." He shook his head. "I don't know why I'm telling you this."

She shrugged. "Maybe because I remind you of someone else. Or maybe because we don't know each other, so it doesn't really matter."

"Maybe."

Their food came. They chatted for another twenty minutes. Cohen looked at his watch. "I've got to get back." He raised his hand to attract the attention of the server. "Check, please."

A few minutes later, the server brought the check. "Let me pay," Cohen said.

"I don't know," Janet replied.

"I insist."

"Only if you let me buy dinner."

"That doesn't seem quite fair."

"I'm the one who's taking advantage of you. I get to enjoy your company instead of eating alone."

Cohen shrugged. "If that's how you really feel."

"I do. Let's trade information. I'll text you later this afternoon."

They exchanged phone numbers.

Cohen stood up. "It's been great talking with you."

"See you tonight."

Cohen paid at the cash register and hurried off. Janet finished her wine. Tonight she'd close the deal. Fine dining, a little too much alcohol, and he'd be in her bed. She'd have all the info they'd need in the next few days.

2

Meanwhile, the contract killers, going by the names Sean and Phyllis, were sitting on the sofa in a hotel suite in Chicago. Sean was a middle-age Black man with close-cropped hair who wore Brooks Brothers suits and conservative neckties. His partner, Phyllis, was a Black woman with a short Afro, who wore dresses and flat shoes. To civilians, they looked like business professionals or church folk. They'd just finished tracking down a bookmaker who'd run off with $50,000 of the Orange Hill Cartel's money. They left him trussed up in the trunk of a Toyota Corolla in the underground parking lot, the key fob on the pavement in front of the rear wheel. Sean ended a call on a burner phone. "That should keep them off our backs for a little while anyway."

"Don't they understand the problem? The grifters have gone to ground somewhere, and until they move, we can't find them."

"Orange Hill doesn't care about our problems. They want results."

"Well, Terry's internet searches—known credit card numbers, public surveillance cameras—have come up empty ever since they disappeared in Nebraska after the Cleveland job," Phyllis replied.

"So they must be hiding out in the upper plains somewhere," Sean said.

His other burner phone was vibrating. "Speak of the devil." He answered the phone and put it on speaker. "What have you got for us, Terry?"

"Spotted the targets on cameras in Rocky Shore, Missouri."

"Passing through?"

"Doesn't look like it."

"We're on our way. Text if anything changes." He ended the call. He put the burner phone in his jacket pocket, took out his smartphone, and opened his map app. "About five hours by car."

"Let's get our gear loaded and get on the road," Phyllis said.

THAT EVENING, after dinner, Janet stood together with Jay Cohen just inside a hotel suite she'd booked earlier in the day, their arms around each other. They kissed and kissed again. Janet unbuttoned his shirt and ran her hand over his chest.

"You sure you want to do this?" Cohen asked.

She looked up into his eyes. "Are *you* sure?"

"Uh-huh." He kissed her again.

She pulled him through to the bedroom, unbuckled his pants and pushed him back on the bed. Then she pulled off her panties and climbed on top of him.

Allen sat on the floor in the front closet, monitoring the camera hidden in the headboard of the bed. He smiled. The marks always fell for it. She was just that good. After tonight, if Cohen decided not to be helpful, they'd find out what he thought of the camera footage.

A LITTLE AFTER 9:00 p.m., the contract killers Sean and Phyllis took the first freeway exit into Rocky Shore, Missouri, and checked into an Embassy Suites motel. As soon as they moved their bags into their suite, Sean called Terry.

"What can you tell us about the grifters?"

"They're driving a red RAV4. Colorado plates. Sometimes they use a rental. They're very active near the surveillance camera by a Walmart on Dixie Boulevard."

"Any particular times of day?"

"Around 8:00 a.m. I'm guessing there's a coffee shop nearby."

"Text me a still of the Walmart surveillance camera."

"You bet."

The text came up on his phone. "Thanks, Terry. Keep us updated." He ended the call.

He turned to Phyllis. "Did you hear that?"

"Yeah. Guess we've got a busy few days."

The next morning, Sean and Phyllis sat in their black Suburban in the Walmart parking lot where they had a clear view of the area that the RAV4 would be driving through. At 8:07 a.m., they watched the RAV4 drive by, the female grifter by herself. They pulled out after her. She got in the drive-through line of a Caffeination Coffee Shop. They pulled into a MacDonald's restaurant across the street.

When she left the coffee shop, they followed her into a neighborhood of single-family homes with well-kept yards. She pulled into the driveway of a house in the middle of a block. They drove by, turned around at the end of the block, and parked on the street with a good view of the house the female grifter had gone in.

"We could take them now," Phyllis said. "Flashbang grenade through the window. Spray the place with gunfire."

"And if they get away, we're starting over. No, we're going to nail them this time, avoid attention from the authorities, and take whatever cash they're carrying."

"They might not be carrying any appreciable amount."

"True," Sean replied. "I'm just assuming they use cash whenever they can. One thing for sure, we don't know what kind of weapons they have in there. We could end up in a gunfight. They could escape through the back. As long as they don't know we're here, we can wait until we can catch them out in the open where they're vulnerable. I don't want them to get away this time."

At 11:30 a.m., the grifters came out of the house and got into the RAV4. Sean and Phyllis followed them downtown, where they parked in an underground parking garage. Phyllis got out of the Suburban and followed them while Sean parked. She didn't know if they knew what she looked like, so she took care not to be seen. At 12:15 p.m., the female grifter, casual dress that clung to her curves, stood in front of Freedom Bank and Trust. A young man with a short beard came out of the bank and gave her a hug. They walked down the street to Big Pop's Barbeque, the male grifter trailing half a block behind. Phyllis stopped at a street corner where the male grifter couldn't see her, stepped back to the building, and got out her phone. A few minutes later, Sean caught up to her.

She put away her phone. "Did you see her new love interest?"

"I did."

"He's already smitten."

"She knows her business."

Sean and Phyllis went back to the parking deck and waited. The grifters came out of the stairwell and drove back out to their house. Sean pulled over at a nearby bus stop. "Ready for lunch?"

"There's a deli near the Walmart," Phyllis said.

"What kind of sandwich do you want?"

"Chicken and Swiss," Phyllis replied. "And an iced tea."

"Okay," Sean said. "Why don't you wait here?"

Phyllis got out and stood at the bus stop. A middle-age woman wearing nursing scrubs came up to the bus stop, nodded, and sat on the bench. The bus came. She got on. Phyllis sat on the bench. A few minutes later, Sean pulled up in the Suburban.

"Anything?"

"No movement."

He parked at the end of the block with a view of the grifters' house. They ate their sandwiches and waited. At 5:00 p.m., the grifters got in their SUV. The female was wearing a party dress that showed all of her to advantage. The male was wearing dark, nondescript clothes. Sean and Phyllis followed them back downtown, taking care not to be seen.

The grifters parked in the parking garage. The female met her love interest in front of the bank. They walked off down the sidewalk, hand-in-hand. The male stood to one side, acting like he was talking on his phone. Phyllis followed the female and her lover, taking care not to be noticed by the male grifter.

Sean stood back at the corner, watching the male grifter. Pedestrians were walking by the bank in a steady flow. Sean put his hand on the Smith & Wesson snub-nose in his jacket pocket. The grifter was focused on the front of the bank. With all the pedestrian churn, Sean could get in the flow, walk by behind him, and shoot him in the back of the head. Boom. Everyone would scatter. He'd be gone before anyone noticed him, and the female would be easy pickings without her man.

He slipped into the pedestrian traffic behind three women in office wear, but when he was about five steps away, a middle-age South Asian dressed like an executive came out of Freedom Bank and Trust carrying a laptop bag, and the male grifter started after him. Was this guy part of the scam? Sean let go of his pistol and took his hand out of his pocket. He'd missed his chance. He wouldn't be able to get close enough while the grifter was moving. He let the grifter and the executive get a block ahead of him and then started after them.

The executive went into an apartment building near an upscale restaurant and shopping area. The grifter went into a coffee shop across the street and took a table where he could watch the apartment building's front door. Sean hung back at the corner, stood at a bus stop for twenty minutes, and then took a chance on circling the block. The grifter was still in place when he got back. Another hour later, the executive, still in his suit, came out of his building. The grifter followed him, and Sean followed the grifter. The executive went into a Hilton Hotel across the street from the convention center. The grifter followed. Sean stood on the street looking in the windows to the hotel. The executive went into the bar. The grifter sat in the lobby.

Sean got out his phone and called Phyllis. "What do you know?"

"They're in a restaurant, all lovey-dovey, so I'm betting it's his place or her place afterward."

"Think he's the mark?"

"He doesn't look rich enough."

"The male's been following an executive who came out of the bank after the love interest. They're in the bar of a Hilton."

"So he's the mark?"

"Time will tell. Why are they seducing the young guy? What does he know or have access to?"

"Does he work for the executive?"

"Let's have Terry investigate the bank. Find out who these people are. Then we'll have a better idea what's going on." He chuckled.

"What's funny?"

"I almost shot the male in front of the bank. Lost my chance."

"He's got to leave the Hilton sometime. You could catch him on the street. Do you want any help?"

"I thought it was a good idea at the time, but now I think we should wait. They're in the middle of a scam. If we wait until they try to take the score, we'll be able to catch them at their most preoccupied, which will give us our greatest advantage. Plus we'll be able to keep their score."

"Could be tricky. If they spot us, we'll be done."

"You're right, we could be, but the extra money could come in handy."

"Okay. I'll go along for now, but if we get an opportunity to kill them, we've got to take it."

"Of course."

"So are we done for tonight?"

"Yeah, I'll meet you back at the parking deck."

THE NEXT DAY Sean and Phyllis arrived at the duplex at 7:55 a.m. The female went for coffee at around 8:00 a.m. The male dropped her at the bank at lunchtime and picked her up after the lover boy went back to work. While they were watching the duplex in the afternoon, they got a call from Terry.

"Hey, guys. I'm texting you the photo directory of the bank's employees. Let me know if you need anything else."

Sean opened the text. He and Phyllis looked through the directory. The executive was Vice President for Trusts Benny Singh. The love interest was his personal assistant, Jay Cohen.

Sean smiled. "So the grifters must be using the personal assistant to gain access to information they need for the scam they're working on Singh."

"That's what it looks like."

"We don't need to follow the female grifter anymore. We need to stay on the male and Singh."

"Unless Cohen has access to all the passwords and equipment," Phyllis said.

"We haven't seen him carrying anything when he leaves the office. Singh leaves with a laptop."

"You think that's the weak link?"

"Yeah, I surely do."

"Okay. But let's keep tracking them both for two more days, just to be sure."

OVER THE NEXT TWO DAYS, the killers continued to track the grifters from 7:00 a.m. to 8:00 p.m. The pattern held. The female went to lunch and dinner with Cohen. The male followed Singh home after work and then to a bar in the neighborhood. Every day Singh carried his laptop home.

"Are you convinced?" Sean asked.

"I am. As soon as the female has the information they need, they'll do whatever they're planning to do to Singh."

"So tomorrow we stop following Cohen. You follow Singh, keeping well back, and I'll trail behind in our Suburban with our gear. When the grifters make their play, we'll take them out while they're focused on their score."

. . .

THE NEXT AFTERNOON, after they'd finished eating an early dinner of takeout Chinese, Sean got a call on his burner phone. It was Mr. Wishes, the Orange Hill Cartel associate who'd hired them. "Are they dead yet?"

Sean looked across the motel suite, thinking carefully about his response. "We're setting up on them now. In the next day or two, the job should be done."

"That's what you said the last two times."

"Look, you called us in because your guys couldn't get it done. You know how hard it is. We want to be done with this job as much as you do. We're going to close just as soon as we can."

"Make it happen."

"Yes, sir."

"Don't let them get away." Mr. Wishes ended the call.

Phyllis walked in from the bedroom. "Was that Mr. Wishes?"

"None other."

"Three's a charm. Did you tell him that?"

"No, and I didn't tell him we've been trying to catch them on the getaway so that we could take their score after we kill them. Haven't charged the Orange Hill Cartel nearly enough for the amount of work it's taken to keep after these grifters."

She sat on the arm of the sofa. "If we don't get them this time, we ought to cut our losses."

"Mr. Wishes isn't going to allow that. Look how he's dogging the grifters. We don't want to get on his bad side." He looked at his watch. "Time to change clothes for the night's work."

"Still want me on Singh?"

"Yes. Whenever the grifters spring their trap, we're going to be ready."

THE GRIFTERS, Allen and Janet, sat on the back deck of their Airbnb drinking coffee.

"So you got Singh's condo password and mutual funds account password from Cohen?"

"Easy peasy. The guy sleeps like a baby drunk on milk. Found them in a daybook in his home office."

"It wasn't that easy. Took the better part of a week."

"Sure, I took it slow. He doesn't suspect a thing."

"And he's not expecting you for dinner tonight?"

"No. Told him my cousin was in town overnight."

Allen nodded. "Singh always takes his laptop home at night?"

"Cohen says always. Likes to work at night and first thing in the morning."

"Makes the embezzlement easier, I suppose."

"Well, Cohen is paying Singh's bills tomorrow, so he's got the maximum amount of cash in his mutual fund account."

"Then I guess tonight's the night. All we have to do is get Singh's right index fingerprint to open his phone and his laptop."

"We've gone over this before," Janet said. "What's bothering you?"

"Sean and Phyllis disrupted our last two jobs. Cost us our payday in Miami. Messed up our getaway in Cleveland."

"You think they're here, waiting for us to move?"

"One time—that could be bad luck. Two times—no. They've got some way of finding us. And as long as the Orange Hill Cartel is paying, they're going to be after us."

"But now we're expecting them."

"You're right. But they're expecting that we're expecting them. We've still got a few dollars in the bank. We could walk away from this score if we needed to. Staying alive and free is more important than this score."

"Or any score."

"Maximum paranoia until we're away clean."

"Always."

"Then let's take Singh's money."

3

At 9:30 p.m., Phyllis, Kevlar vest under her raincoat, stood on the street outside the Hilton Hotel a few blocks from Singh's condo, her phone to her ear as if she was in the midst of a conversation. She'd followed Singh from his condo to the Hilton bar. Sean was tracking the male grifter. She turned to the wall as the female grifter, dolled up in a gold-colored cocktail dress and short black jacket, a handbag over one shoulder, went into the Hilton. Phyllis watched through the glass as the grifter stepped through to the bar. She called Sean. "The female is making a move."

"The male is parked on the street two blocks away."

THE HILTON BAR was busy with the convention crowd. Janet spotted Singh near the end of the bar in a quiet conversation with a woman who was obviously a call girl, their faces close together as they talked. Janet squeezed up to the bar on the other side of Singh. He glanced at her as she bumped his shoulder, then turned back to his companion. The bartender came down to her, and she ordered a glass of white wine.

She glanced at Singh's drink. It was golden brown with one oversize ice cube. Probably an Old Fashioned. She took a small dropper bottle out of her handbag and palmed it. She was watching the call girl out of the corner of her eye. The bartender brought Janet her drink. She smiled and set a credit card on the bar. The bartender picked it up. Just then, she saw the bartender and the call girl exchange a glance. Was Singh a bigger fool than he appeared to be? Were they working him together? Or did Singh even care?

The call girl kissed him, a quick peck on the lips, and walked away. He turned to watch her. Janet glanced at the bartender. He was busy at the other end of the bar. She pulled the tip from the dropper and squeezed three drops into Singh's drink. Then she capped the dropper and put it back in her handbag. The bartender came back down the bar with her bill and her credit card. She signed, put her card away, and took a sip of her drink.

Singh turned back to the bar, swirled his drink, and took a gulp. He looked disappointed. Then he glanced at Janet again.

"Hello," he said.

"Hello."

"I haven't seen you here before. You with a convention?"

"Where did your friend go?"

"Old friend." He took another gulp of his drink. "Not what you think. We have a lot of history, but no future."

Janet smiled. "What's your name?"

"Benny Singh. I live around the corner."

"Downtown?"

"Yes. This is my watering hole."

"So you must be in finance or banking or something like that."

"Why do you say that?"

"Because those are the only people who can afford to live down here."

"Touché. I'm a banker. What do you do?"

"I'm retired."

"You're awfully young to be retired."

"Now you're flirting."

He smiled. His eyes were glassy, and he was starting to sway ever so slightly on his seat.

"Are you okay, Benny?"

"I'm feeling suddenly under the weather."

"Is it your heart? Do you need an ambulance?"

"No, no. I just need to get home."

"Let me help you."

"I don't know. I wouldn't want to put you out."

"It's no problem. Really."

He stood up. She took him by the elbow and led him out onto the street.

"I'm crazy dizzy for some reason."

"You need to lie down. Which way?"

"That way." He pointed to the left.

She led him down the street, walking along as if she didn't already know where his building was.

"I really appreciate your help."

"You're not playing a game, are you?"

"What do you mean?"

"Trying to lure me to your apartment?"

"No, no, no." He staggered toward the street. "I mean, you're a beautiful lady, but—"

"Careful," she said. She pulled him back to the center of the sidewalk.

They came to the door to his building. While Singh pulled a fob out of his pocket and touched the reader, Janet slipped on a pair of throwaway gloves. The door buzzed. Janet opened it and led Singh into the lobby. The doorman was not behind the desk. They went to the elevator and used the fob to go up to the eighth floor. He was wobbling back and forth as they moved down the hall to his apartment. After two tries, he managed to enter his alarm code correctly.

Janet led him into his apartment, passed through the living room to his bedroom, and pushed him over onto his bed face up. His arm flopped over. His eyes shut. She put his legs up on the bed and took off his shoes. He started to snore. She felt his neck for a pulse. It was strong.

She took a square of foil, a cigarette lighter, a glue stick, and a tiny bottle of wood glue from her handbag and set them on the night table next to Singh's bed. Then she warmed the glue stick with the lighter and put two dabs on the foil. She lifted Singh's right hand, licked his index fingertip, and pressed the fingertip into both dabs of glue stick glue. She lay Singh's hand next to his body and then examined the reverse fingerprints she'd made. They looked good. She dripped some wood glue onto the reverse fingerprints and then put her supplies back into her handbag.

She glanced at Singh. He was still out cold. She took his smartphone from his front pants pocket and dropped it into her jacket pocket. Then she picked up the square of foil and blew on the wood glue to dry it before she carried the square of foil into Singh's home office and set it down next to his computer.

She called Allen. "I'm in."

"All good?" Allen asked.

"We'll know in a few minutes."

"Let me know if you need anything."

PHYLLIS STOOD on the sidewalk across the street from Singh's building, which stood on a quiet side street. She got out her phone and called Sean. "Female took Singh upstairs. Looks like he's doped."

"Male is sitting tight for now," Sean replied. "I'm moving down towards you. Where's the stairwell door to the street, just in case she doesn't come down the elevator?"

Phyllis glanced down the block. "Three storefronts down, between a dry cleaner's and a shoe repair place."

"Is there a place for me to park on the near side of Singh's building's main entrance?"

"An empty metered spot on the right."

"I'm on the move."

. . .

JANET SAT in the dark at the desk in Singh's home office, looking at the screen of Singh's laptop computer. The wood glue was dry. She peeled the wood glue off the reverse fingerprints to create the positive fingerprints. The second looked slightly better than the first. She used the fingerprint mold to unlock Singh's computer. When the screen asked for verification, she chose telephone response, then she used Singh's fingerprint to open his phone and verify the user. She smiled to herself. Couldn't be easier. She opened Singh's browser, went through his bookmarks and opened his personal brokerage account. Over three million dollars in mutual funds, but only $200,723 in cash. It was less money than they'd hoped for, but it was too difficult to move the mutual funds quickly, so they'd have to settle for the cash.

She took a scrap of paper from her pocket and input the routing instructions to move the cash to the First National Bank of Northern Utah in Provo, Utah. Then she closed the laptop, put the fingerprint mold in her pocket, and went back into the bedroom, where she slipped Singh's phone back in his front pants pocket. She checked his pulse again. Still strong.

She reset Singh's security system before she left. She took out her smartphone as she walked down the hallway and clicked on Allen's phone number. "I'm coming down."

"I'll be at the door."

She pulled a red wig out of her handbag and set it sloppily on her head before she pushed through the fire door to the stairwell. When she spotted the surveillance camera at the ceiling on the next landing, she held her hand up in front of her face.

Allen was waiting in the RAV4 when she came out of the stairwell. The street was quiet and dark. She climbed into the passenger's seat.

"Any difficulty?"

"Like clockwork," Janet said.

"With any kind of luck," Allen said, "we'll be long gone before he knows what happened."

As he put the RAV4 into drive, a gun boomed and the back

window of the SUV shattered. He ducked in the seat and pushed the gas petal to the floor. "Seatbelt," he yelled. They sped away for the curb.

Another shot rang out but missed the SUV. Allen sat up. "What can you see?"

Janet engaged her seatbelt and stuck her head out the passenger's side window. "Guy climbing into the passenger side of a black Suburban. They're after us."

Allen careened right around the next corner, sped down the street, and slid around to the left at the next stop sign.

"Is it Sean and Phyllis?"

"Too dark to tell. The guy was black, though."

"Meaning it was Sean. Him shooting and Phyllis driving. We've got to do something about them."

"Let's get out of here first. I don't want to get into a shootout on the street."

Allen took the ramp onto the beltway, drove two exits, and then got off onto a surface street. "Still back there?"

"I think we lost them."

"It's just about two-thirty," Allen said. "Let's circle around for a few hours and then go to the airport."

"I don't know, babe. Airports are full of cameras and cops."

"True. But Sean and Phyllis can't just walk in with weapons."

"Still don't want to go. We might be on a watch list."

"I think our ID's will hold up. We need to get a head start on Sean and Phyllis. They always seem to catch up with us after we get started on a job. They must be hacking into public surveillance cameras."

"You're saying they've got a hacker using some sort of AI program to hunt for us?"

"It's the only thing that makes sense. That's why they can't find us when we're hiding. If we take a plane, they won't know where we're landing, which should buy us extra time to escape."

"Maybe. Maybe their hacker can hack inside the airport."

"Maybe. At this point I'm just rolling the dice and hoping our luck holds out."

"As least we got paid this time."

"Got to be alive to spend the money."

"Okay, fingers crossed, the airport it is. Where we flying to?"

"Las Vegas. Not too far from Provo and the money, but far enough that we could be going in a lot of different directions."

Janet took out her phone and bought tickets on the next available flight.

They drove surface streets, circling randomly, until a line of dawn broke pink at the horizon. Allen parked on a side street next to a hotel across the street from the Rocky Shore Airport. They wiped down the SUV, dropped their pistols down the storm drain at the corner, pulled off their throwaway gloves, and walked around to the front of the hotel. They stood to one side of the door to the lobby and waited for the airport shuttle. When it came, they got on it just as if they'd been staying at the hotel. Three other travelers and an airplane pilot and two flight attendants got on before the shuttle pulled away.

Twenty minutes later, the shuttle stopped in front of the Departures doors at the airport. The area in front of the ticket counters was mostly empty. Janet stopped and grabbed Allen's arm. "You sure this is the best plan? We're leaving everything behind."

"Sean and Phyllis knew where we were going to be, so they probably know where we've been staying. It's the most obvious place to ambush us. No matter what we do, we can't go back to the Airbnb."

"We could just pick up a rental car and get on the freeway."

"Too easy for a hacker to track us. Cameras at the rental car place. Cameras at every convenience store. We fly out of here and they're starting from scratch trying to find us."

"Maybe."

"It's a better chance than driving away from here when we know Sean and Phyllis are right behind us."

"Let's give Billy a call. See if he has more details about our situation."

"Fair enough. Let's step away from the door." Allen took out his smartphone, speed- dialed Billy, and put it on speaker. "Hey, buddy, sorry to call so early. Is there anything new about our problem?"

"Last I heard is that an Orange Hill gangster who goes by Mr. Wishes has put you at the top of his to-do list. The contractors work for him."

"These names. I guess they think it makes them sound scary."

"Scary enough for me, brother. You know this guy?"

"We know him. Any specifics?"

"That's all. He's hard after you two."

"Let us know if you hear anything else."

"Will do."

He ended the call. "So it's Mr. Wishes. Could it be any worse?"

"I'm a little surprised that he's still holding a grudge for the diamonds and the cash."

"Well, we did poke him in the eye twice."

"There wasn't that much money involved."

"That's not how he'd look at it. Ready to take a plane?"

SEAN SAT behind the wheel in their black Suburban at the beginning of the drop-off zone at the departures area at the airport. Cars were pulling up to the curb, dropping passengers for the 6:00 a.m. flight. Phyllis hurried over to the Suburban and climbed in. "The grifters are in line to go through security," she said. "What do you want to do?"

"We're not going in there empty-handed. Be our luck to get murdered in the airport. Let's see if we can get some eyes on them." He made a phone call and put it on speaker.

"Hello?"

"Hey, Terry. I need eyes on our targets inside the airport. They're in the TSA line right now."

"Jesus, how about a little notice?"

"You picked them up on the outside camera here. What did you think was going to happen?"

"I'll call you back in a few minutes." He ended the call.

"Now we wait," Sean said.

"If it's a ruse and they come back out, how far do we let them go before we kill them?"

"I doubt if they're carrying their score—wouldn't want to pack it through the airport—so we won't be able to take it. They're not armed, or they wouldn't be in the TSA line. This would be an excellent opportunity. This time of the day, we could drop them on the sidewalk in front of the terminal for all I care. We'd be long gone before the police got here."

Terry called back. "Okay, I'm on the airport cameras. No mean feat, I'm telling you. These computer system upgrades are a pain in the ass."

"Pat yourself on the back," Sean said.

"Targets have cleared security. Going to their gate. Hang on a minute. I'm switching cameras to follow them."

The line was quiet for a few minutes. "You there?"

"Yeah."

"They're sitting at gate C23, 6:15 a.m. to Las Vegas."

"Call us back when they get on the plane." Sean ended the call. He turned to Phyllis. "Do you want a cup of coffee?"

"I'd love one."

Sean pulled away from the curb and drove to a Perkins restaurant anchoring a strip mall across the street from the airport. They sat in a booth and ordered coffee. He set his phone on the table. They were finishing their second cup when the phone rang.

"Yeah?"

"Doors closed on the plane. They're headed to Las Vegas."

"Hack the Las Vegas cameras. I want to know if someone picks them up or if they rent a car—whatever they do, I want to know it."

"Will do."

Phyllis motioned to their server and got the check. Sean left money on the table. When they got into their Suburban, he called Mr. Wishes and put it on speaker.

"Good news, I hope?"

"They escaped. They're on the first flight to Las Vegas."

"How did they manage that? Wait, don't bother. I'm not interested in your excuses. I'm beginning to think it was a mistake hiring you."

"Every time out, we're getting closer."

"That's not comforting. What are your next steps?"

"My hacker is going to shadow them until we can catch up. We'll blast them away in a crowd if we have to."

"See that you do." He ended the call.

"When's the next flight?" Sean asked.

Phyllis opened a travel app on her phone. "Plane leaves in three hours."

"That's a long head start."

"That's all there is."

"Are there two seats?"

"In first class."

"Book them."

"Done."

Sean pulled out of the Perkins parking lot. "What we're doing is not working. We need a plan that's better than chasing them down and hoping to kill them before they find out we're after them."

"But that's what you told Mr. Wishes we would do."

"That's what he expected to hear."

"If we gave up trying to take their score, we'd have more options," Phyllis said.

"There's no way the Orange Hill Cartel is going to cover all our expenses."

"Because they think we've been incompetent?"

"Because they're assholes and know they don't have to pay. But maybe you're right. Maybe we should just murder the grifters and take a loss."

"Have you got any ideas on how to get ahead of them?"

"Nothing yet," Sean said. "The first step is to keep them in our sights."

4

After Allen and Janet landed at the Harry Reid International Airport in Las Vegas, they rented a white Toyota Corolla at the Enterprise Rent-A-Car and started up Interstate 15 north toward Provo, Utah. The traffic thinned out rapidly as they left the suburbs.

"We've got to find a way to get Orange Hill off our backs for good," Allen said.

"Mr. Wishes is the one who wants us," Janet replied.

"We need to go on the offensive."

"That's a dangerous idea, baby."

"We've been playing defense. It's getting us nowhere. We make a mistake at the wrong time just once, and we're done. And if we kill Sean and Phyllis, Mr. Wishes is just going to send someone else. Orange Hill isn't going to stop chasing us until they can't chase us anymore."

"So how are we going to stop them? They're too big for us to take on by ourselves, and if we try to put another cartel on them, they'll probably just capture us and sell us to Orange Hill."

"What about setting the Feds on them?" Allen moved to the left lane and passed a semitruck.

"After the jail break in Ohio? They'd just as soon arrest us as help us with the Orange Hill Cartel."

"What about the National Defense Agency?"

"Garcia wasn't too happy with you targeting her rogue agent."

"Yeah, but she didn't arrest me or try to kill me."

"So you want to put Garcia and the NDA on Mr. Wishes?"

"I want to clear a big payday, get the Orange Hill Cartel off our backs, and have Garcia owing us a favor."

"Honey, I love your optimism, but we've just scored $200,000. We could run a long time."

"There's no future in running. Sean and Phyllis will just find us again in a couple of months."

"Okay, let's say we try to disrupt Orange Hill's operations."

"Let's focus on Mr. Wishes. He's the one who's after us," Allen said.

"Okay, Mr. Wishes. To get the NDA involved, we'd need a target that will pass muster as a national security threat."

"True."

"And we can't dig into his business ourselves."

"Let's see if Billy can help us out."

Allen took out his smartphone and put it on speaker. "Billy?"

"What can I do for you?"

"Two things. First, we need guns."

"How soon?"

"Immediately."

"Where are you?"

"In Nevada, headed toward Provo, Utah."

"I'll get back to you on that. What else?"

"We need to get the Orange Hill Cartel off our backs. Can you make some discreet inquires into any big projects Mr. Wishes might be involved in?"

"I can't promise anything, but I might have a couple of leads."

"That's all we're asking."

"I'll be in touch."

. . .

AT 11:30 A.M., Olivia Blevins, Singh's second in command, used her fob to get into Singh's building and took the elevator up to the eighth floor. She rang the bell on Singh's condo and listened for footsteps. Nothing. She rang the bell again. A housekeeper came out of the condo across the hall and glanced at her as she started toward the elevator. Olivia banged on the door with her fist, but no one opened it. Finally, she dug the door keys out of her bag. That's when the door opened.

Singh stood there, disheveled, still dressed in the suit he'd been wearing the day before, his hair tousled and his face unshaved. "Why are you here so early?"

"Early?" She stepped past him into the entryway. "It's after eleven."

He turned from the door. "What are you talking about?"

"Christ, what happened to you? You're a mess. I've been calling all morning."

She shut the door and led him into the living room. "Where were you last night?"

He sat on the sofa and rubbed his face with his hands. "The last thing I remember was having a drink at the bar in the Hilton."

"You weren't taking drugs?"

"No, of course not, not since before rehab last year."

"Do you have your wallet?"

He felt his back pocket. "Yes."

"Your money and credit cards?"

He took out his wallet and looked. "Everything is here." He tossed the wallet onto the coffee table.

"Your phone?"

He pulled it out of his front pocket and laid it on the coffee table.

"You missed a ten o'clock with Jacob Meir. That's what got me worried."

"How mad was he?"

"I covered for you. Said you had food poisoning."

"God, I feel like death."

"Take a shower. I'll make some coffee."

Singh took a quick shower and changed clothes. He was knotting his necktie as he came back into the living room. Olivia handed him a cup of black coffee.

"Feel better?"

"A little."

"Can you remember anything more?"

"No."

"You must have gotten home somehow."

He shook his head. "I've got nothing."

"Let's look at your front door camera."

He picked up his smartphone and opened his security system app.

"Hand it to me." Olivia looked at the timeline. "You got here at ten-thirty." She showed him the blurry video footage of him stumbling in the door with a woman. "Who is she?"

"I don't know. I don't remember."

"Somebody came in here with you."

"That's not possible."

"The camera doesn't lie. Either she's a date or she roofied you to break into your house."

"That's crazy."

"Is your work computer here?"

He nodded. They went into his home office. The desk, the chair, the open laptop computer—everything was just as he had left it when he went out.

"Open your computer and check your mutual fund account," she said.

He used his index fingerprint to wake up the computer, opened his brokerage account, and used his phone to verify his identity. The cash account was empty.

"No way, no way, no way," he said. "Over $200,000 is missing." He clicked through several screens in his account to be sure he wasn't misreading. "Damn it."

"So that explains it," Olivia said. "They couldn't get into your account without your fingerprint and phone. Who knows about this account, besides me?"

"The basic information is on the desktop in Jay's office. He'd know, a few of the analysts would know, that's about it."

"Are there cameras in the lobby?"

"Of course."

"Let's see what they show."

They rode the elevator down to the lobby. The day doorman was sorting mail. "Larry," Singh said. "I'd like to see the surveillance footage from ten-thirty last night."

"Sure, Mr. Singh, come on back."

He led them through a doorway to a small room where an Ikea desk was outfitted with a desktop computer. "I'll pull it up."

He opened the surveillance video footage and put it in reverse at high speed, watching the time marker on the bottom. He stopped the feed at 10:20 p.m. and put it on forward. A few minutes later they saw Singh and a woman in a gold-colored cocktail dress enter the lobby and take the elevator. They couldn't see the woman's face.

Larry turned to Singh and Olivia. "Was this what you were looking for?"

"Who's on duty at ten-thirty?" Singh asked.

"Christian. But he would have been in the alley, organizing the garbage."

"So no one is guarding the door?"

"As you know, the door is locked from nine p.m. on. Either you use your fob, or you have to be buzzed in."

"So someone would have to ring the bell if they didn't have a fob?"

"Yep. Then Christian would have come. Otherwise, residents are on their own."

"Thanks, Larry."

"Is there some problem? Do you need me to call the police?"

"No, no worries. Forget we ever talked about this."

Singh and Olivia went back up to his condo.

"They broke into my house and stole $200,000 from my account," Singh said. "How much do they know?"

"Do you mean, do they know we've been skimming the trust accounts? I don't know," Olivia said. "It seems they had reason to believe that you can't go to the cops. Open your account again."

He opened his brokerage account. Olivia moved through some screens. "They moved the money to an account at the First National Bank of Northern Utah in Provo."

"Can we get it back from here?"

She shook her head. "You know how it works. The process is too far along. That money's gone."

He walked over to the window and looked down at the traffic on the street. Then he turned back to Olivia. "Can't we get it back the same way they got it?"

"You mean have them transfer it back into your account?"

"Exactly."

"Force them to open their account and move the money? We'd have to capture them and put enough pressure on them to get them to do it. That would be hard to do."

"You need to be paid. Carl needs to be paid. And I need cash to pay my bills. We can't just pull another $200,000 from the trust accounts all at once. That would be too suspicious."

"What about converting mutual funds into cash?"

"I can't do that without losing money on the transactions. I'd rather try to get the money back."

"I think it's risky," Olivia said. "But it's your call."

"If we can do it quickly, it's the best option right now."

"How do you want to do it?"

"Let's use a couple of our people from Elemental Security. They're all vetted and loyal."

"Okay, how about we put Barney and Robin on it? They're our best investigators, and they won't flinch at doing what we want done."

Singh nodded. "Dido can oversee them."

"Okay, then, I'll take care of it." Olivia started toward the door.

"Pull yourself together. Eat something. Come into the office after lunch."

SINGH WENT into his living room and sat on his sofa. If thieves could just steal from his personal mutual fund account at will, he didn't have any security at all. Whoever had his phone and his fingerprint could gain access to his computer. He had to be more careful. What a mess. He couldn't afford to lose that money. Alimony, child support, school fees, property taxes, two mortgages—he was being bled to death.

He'd always been willing to take too many risks. Sleeping with that intern and then not offering her a job. Who'd have thought she'd tell his wife? Who'd have thought his wife knew about the others?

Then borrowing money from a trust fund to keep his bills paid. He paid it back the first few times, but it was so easy to transfer the money, and with so many ups and downs in the stock market, easy to cover up the missing cash. By the time Olivia figured out what he was doing, it was too late to back out. He needed the extra money and Olivia wanted a taste. Then Carl Thompson, the bank examiner, noticed the discrepancies when he audited the books, and he had to be dealt with. Singh wasn't sure how Olivia managed that, but it had become another ongoing expense.

But now? Someone knew what he was up to. Or maybe he was just low hanging fruit. Maybe they didn't know anything and came after his mutual fund account because they could. Either way, they needed to be taught a lesson and he needed his money back.

But who really knew what was going on? He, Olivia, and Carl. Olivia was beyond reproach. But Carl, what did they really know about him except that he would take a bribe to ignore the altered paperwork in the trust accounts. Still, Carl had as much to lose as they did. If word got out, he'd be fired, arrested, and jailed. Just like Olivia and him. Plus, Carl would never get another job working around financial records. All of which made it highly unlikely that he would tell anyone.

Singh went into the kitchen, put a bagel in the toaster, and got the cream cheese out of the refrigerator. Dido, Barney, and Robin would sort this out. But the real issue was changing his security so that it couldn't happen again.

WHEN THE CONTRACT killers Sean and Phyllis came out onto the sidewalk in front of the Las Vegas International airport, a silver Toyota Highlander honked its horn at them, and a Latino wearing blue work clothes got out of the driver's side.

Sean's phone vibrated. He had a text. *The Highlander is yours. Full kit in the back.* He glanced at Phyllis. "That's us."

The Latino handed him the car fob and walked away. They put their roller bags in the back next to two large duffels and drove out of the airport. Phyllis called Terry and put the phone on speaker.

"Tell me something good," she said.

"Targets left Enterprise Rent-A-Car in a white Toyota Corolla. Caught them on cameras on Interstate 15 north. I'll be in touch when they stop anywhere."

"Thanks, Terry."

5

It was after 7:00 p.m. when the Travelers, Allen and Janet, arrived in Provo, Utah. They took an exit near Brigham Young University and got a room in a Best Western motel before they drove down Freedom Boulevard to an Applebee's Restaurant. The parking lot was half empty. They parked with a good view of the front of the restaurant and the parking lot entrance. Inside, they asked for a booth against the far wall where they could watch the doors.

"No one could possibly be after us yet," Janet said.

"Belt and suspenders, honey."

She looked in her menu. "What are you going to have?"

"I'm going to get a burger and a salad. And a Coke."

"A Coke?"

"Just want to fit in. Not drinking coffee, tea, or alcohol in Mormon territory."

"I'm going for the salmon and rice pilaf."

While they ate, two couples came in and were seated in booths by the front windows and a man came in and sat that the bar. "Civilians," Allen said.

"What did I tell you?" Janet replied. "No one has had time to catch up with us yet."

As they were crossing the parking lot to their car, Allen's phone rang. It was Billy.

"What have you got for us?"

"Found a gun guy. He'll meet you in the parking lot on Stadium Avenue near Brigham Young University football stadium in forty minutes. He'll be in a Bronco. He's not a cop, but he's an oddball. Watch your back."

"Anything on Orange Hill yet?"

"It's going to take some time."

"Thanks, Billy." Allen turned to Janet. "Did you hear all that?"

"Uh-huh." Janet clicked on the map app on her phone. "Not far, maybe ten minutes tops."

"Let's drive around a few minutes. Get a feel for the streets in case the meet goes wrong."

They left the Applebee's, drove south to Cougar Avenue, took a left, and then took another left onto North University Avenue, drove by South University Parkway, and turned right on Stadium Avenue.

"North University or South University would get us out of here in a hurry," Janet said.

"South University has more lanes, which means the cops could drive faster."

"North University it is."

"Let's hope this guy's not crazy."

A few scattered cars were parked on the stadium side of the Brigham Young University football stadium parking lot. The Bronco sat in the northeast corner. Allen parked next to the Bronco, and he and Janet got out. A leathery-skinned man wearing a frayed cowboy hat and badly worn snakeskin boots got out of the Bronco.

"Do you know Billy?" Allen asked.

The man nodded. "Know him a little. Here to do business. Come on back and see what I got."

The man went around to the back of the Bronco and raised the liftback. A battered Smith & Wesson police special, two Glocks, and a Smith & Wesson hammerless featherweight lay on a ratty blanket. Allen handled each of the pistols in turn.

"These guns have seen a lot of use," he said.

"But they can stand up to a police check. Beggers can't be choosers."

"You got ammunition?"

"Full clip for the Glocks, twelve rounds for each of the others."

Allen turned to Janet. "I'll take whichever of the Glocks is better," she said.

"Okay," Allen said. "We'll take the police special and the Glock on the left."

They argued about the price for a few minutes, then Janet paid in one-hundred-dollar bills. They picked up the pistols. The man opened a tackle box and took out the ammunition.

"Don't load them until I'm gone."

They stood behind their car and watched the man drive out of the parking lot. "That went about as well as expected," Allen said.

"If the guns don't blow up when we fire them," Janet replied.

"We'll get better equipment after we get to a safehouse."

They sat in the car and loaded their pistols before they drove back to the Best Western, where they bought toothbrushes and toothpaste from the convenience store in the lobby on their way up to their room.

Janet kicked off her high heels into the closet. "I hate wearing underwear two days in a row."

Allen took off his shirt and pants and hung them up. "Wash them in the sink and dry them with the hair dryer."

"Too much work."

He smiled. "You could always go commando."

"In a dress this short? No way."

"We'll go shopping first thing after we go to the bank tomorrow."

"You going to shower?"

"In the morning. I'm beat. We've been up since yesterday."

"Slept on the plane and had a cat nap in the car."

"All true. Just not enough."

Janet pushed the curtain aside and peeked out of the window into the parking lot. "What do you think of our chances now?"

"Of outrunning Sean and Phyllis or dealing with Orange Hill?"

"Either or."

"Right now, I think our chances are excellent. But my thinking might change if Sean and Phyllis catch up to us too quickly."

SEAN AND PHYLLIS pulled off the interstate and into a Love's truck stop, where they filled the Highlander's gas tank. Then Sean drove out to the far edge of the lot. "Let's have a look in those duffels."

He raised the liftback, pulled the righthand duffel toward himself, and unzipped it. Two mini machine guns, six magazines of ammunition, two silencers. Phyllis, standing beside him, nodded. "What about the other one?"

Sean zipped that duffel shut and opened the one on his left. Two Glocks, six magazines, two silencers, and a box containing four magnetic tracking devices. "These should do the trick," he said.

A few minutes later, as they drove north on I-15, Phyllis got a call from Terry. She put her phone on speaker. "Targets got off in Provo, Utah. I'll know if their car gets back on the interstate, and I'm trying to track them in town using photo recognition on all public surveillance cameras, but it's hit or miss."

"Keep looking," Sean said.

"Will do."

Phyllis ended the call. "What's our plan? Are we running and gunning?"

"We're still three hours behind them. If we drive all the way to Provo, then get up early, maybe Terry will have something for us, and we'll be after them in real time."

ALLEN AND JANET got up a little after 8:00 a.m., checked out of the Best Western motel, and drove down the street to the Biscuit Man Diner. The diner held a mix of worker and student types, a lot of whom were drinking coffee. Allen had the breakfast special—eggs, pancakes, and sausage—while Janet had yogurt and granola with berries. "We've got a busy day today," Allen said. "We can start collecting the cash we need to stay off the grid, buy some clothes, replace the tech we left in Rocky Shore."

"And get rid of the rental car."

Allen nodded. "If we get all the details right, we're going to be hard to find."

Janet sipped her coffee. "One step at a time."

At 10:00 a.m. they pulled into a branch of the First National Bank of Northern Utah located across from a grocery store in a strip mall. Two cars were parked in front of the bank. A woman wearing business casual came out of the bank and got into one of the cars.

"Nice and quiet," Allen said.

"Just the way we like it," Janet replied.

"How many branches does this bank have?" Allen asked.

"Four, I think."

Allen put on a cap and walked into the bank. There were two tellers behind the counter and a personal banker at a desk in a glass-walled room to the side talking with a man in blue work clothes. Allen went up the counter and took a bank card from his wallet.

"How can I help you?" the teller asked.

"I'd like to withdraw $5,000, please."

"Would you like a check?"

"No, I'd like it in hundreds, please."

"Swipe your card."

He swiped the card.

"Mr. Bixby. This is such a large transaction, could you show some form of ID?"

Allen got out his Tom Bixby driver's license.

"Thank you."

The teller went away and came back with a banded bundle of one-hundred-dollar bills. She broke the band and counted out fifty bills twice. "Would you like an envelope?"

"Thank you."

She put the money in an envelope and passed it to him.

"Thanks."

Allen walked back to the car. Janet was in the middle of a Google search on her smartphone. "Bixby identity is solid," Allen said

Janet glanced up. "I was sure it would stand up."

"Me too. But you don't know for certain until you have to use it."

"Okay," Janet said. "So far as replacing our gear, there're a few shopping malls here. Shops at Riverwoods appears to be the best bet."

"Set a course on your map app."

At the Shops at Riverwoods, they moved quickly between the stores, buying carry-on roller bags, seven days of clothing, and toiletries. They paid with their Bixby First National Bank of Northern Utah Visa card.

"Okay, now we need to go to a beauty supply store," Janet said. She did another Google search. "Found one."

They drove north from Provo to Orem, Utah. The Cosmo Prof beauty supply store was in a strip mall across from a Waffle House restaurant. Janet went in and bought two wigs—one blonde and one black—as well as various shades of liquid foundation.

"You get everything?" Allen asked.

"Yes."

"Okay. There's a Best Buy across town."

"That'll work," Janet said. She used her phone to route them to the Best Buy. They parked in a corner of the parking lot away from the surveillance cameras. "Should we use a new credit card?"

"Let's stick with the Bixby credit card for now," Allen replied. "We don't want anyone who's chasing us to get any new information."

They put on ball caps and went into the store. "I'll get the laptop," Janet said. "You get the cameras."

Allen nodded. "Meet you at checkout."

Allen went into the home security section of the store and picked out three security cameras with built-in audio that didn't require a cell phone plan. Janet met him at the cash registers. "What did you get?" he asked.

"MacBook Air. Plenty of storage for what we need. What about the cameras?"

"More than adequate."

They paid and went back out to their car.

"Okay," Allen said. "Let's go to one more bank, then we'll buy a used car, return this rental, and get out of town."

They found a First National Bank of Northern Utah branch in Orem, and Janet put on the blonde wig and went inside. Ten minutes later, she came back with $5,000.

"Any trouble?"

"None. Told them I need cash to pay a painting contractor."

"There's a CarMax north of here near an Enterprise car rental."

"Let's do it."

In the CarMax lot, they found a used 2015 Ford Focus with 115,000 miles on it. They bargained down the sales manager to $9,500, tax included, and paid with their First National Bank debit card, after a phone call to the bank to adjust the card limit to make the purchase. Then they drove to the Enterprise Rent a Car, returned the rental, and drove away in the Ford Focus.

"Where next?" Janet asked.

"There's a First National Bank of Northern Utah branch in Salt Lake City. Let's drive up there, spend the night, and go to the bank in the morning."

"Okay. And after that, what do we do next? Stay on the move in remote areas where there aren't any surveillance cameras until Billy gets back to us?"

He nodded. "Unfortunately, that's all we've got."

SEAN AND PHYLLIS were sitting at an umbrella table on the patio of a Caffeination coffee shop when Terry called. Sean put his phone on speaker. "It went slower than I wanted, but I found the targets' car on a strip mall camera parked in front of the First National Bank of Northern Utah. After that, I found them at a shopping mall and then another First National Bank, this time in Orem. But the kicker is I got them returning the Corolla to an Enterprise."

"What did they leave in?" Sean asked.

"A red Ford Focus. This was just a couple of minutes ago. They're headed north on I-15."

"Keep after them."

"Of course."

Sean and Phyllis hurried to their Highlander. Sean got into the driver's seat. "Plot the quickest route to I-15 north."

BACK IN ROCKY SHORE, Missouri, Dido, the manager at Elemental Security, sat in her home office, working at her desktop computer. She'd been through all the surveillance video footage inside and outside of the First National Bank of Northern Utah in Provo. She'd captured pictures of a man accessing the account that held the $200,000 and an even better picture of him going into the bank. From the non-encrypted files, she'd gotten the names on the account, Tom and Ruby Bixby, and a home address. She'd pulled up the home in the county property records. The address was a fake. She went back to the outside surveillance footage. She saw Tom Bixby get into a white Toyota Corolla with Nevada license plates.

She went to the security camera feeds at the car rental places outside the Harry Reid International Airport in Las Vegas. Guesstimating back from when the Bixbys must have left town and the flight time to Las Vegas, she started checking the feeds. Thirty minutes later, she spotted the Corolla coming out of the Enterprise Rent-A-Car lot.

Her phone rang. She looked at the screen. It was Barney.

"We're in Provo. What have you got?"

"So far? Tom and Ruby Bixby. Names might be aliases. Home address is fake. They're driving a white Toyota Corolla with Nevada plates. Got it from an Enterprise car rental." She recited the license number.

"That's all?"

"Still working. They were at a First National Bank of Northern Utah branch at ten a.m."

"We'll head toward the branch. Keep us informed."

Dido hacked into the public surveillance cameras and watched the Corolla drive through an intersection two blocks from the bank, heading north. Then she lost it. She hopscotched through the cameras, spreading her radius, but she didn't find the Corolla again. How long would the Bixbys stay in town? They'd come out of the airport without any luggage. They'd have to buy everything, unless they had a safehouse here. So they'd have to go to a shopping center or a strip mall. Restaurants. If they had any sense, they'd switch cars. Then they'd keep moving, get as far away from the First National Bank as they could.

Enterprise. She googled the nearby Enterprise locations and hacked into their cameras one by one, looking for the Bixbys or the Corolla. At the third location, she found them. After he dropped off the Corolla, Bixby got into a red Ford Focus. She zoomed in on the license plate number and copied it. She looked at the time stamp. Two hours ago.

She called Barney. "They switched cars. They're in a red Ford Focus. Here's the license plate number."

He wrote it down.

"I'm guessing that they left town," Dido said.

"Why?"

"It's the smart move."

"I don't know if they're that smart."

"Well, you cruise the motels with good access to the freeway. I'm going to hack into the surveillance cameras along the interstate."

By 8:00 p.m., Dido found them on a surveillance feed on Interstate 15 North. She called Barney. "They were at a rest stop on I-15 headed to Salt Lake City at four this afternoon."

"Crap. That's a four-hour head start."

"I'll start checking surveillance cameras up at Salt Lake. See if they stopped there for the night."

"Okay. We'll drive to Salt Lake and wait for your call when we get there."

ALLEN AND JANET were in a third-floor room at a Holiday Inn Express off Interstate 15 in Salt Lake City. Allen was sitting on the bed fully dressed and watching the local news, the police special lying on the bed beside him.

Janet came out of the bathroom in her underwear. "I really needed that shower."

"Feels good to be clean."

"You're dressed."

"Yeah."

"And you've propped a chair under the doorknob."

"I'm a little surprised that Sean and Phyllis haven't caught up to us."

Janet went to the window and pulled aside the edge of the curtain. The parking lot was well lit, full of cars, and quiet. "I think we've still got a twelve- or fourteen-hour head start."

"I don't know. We've been around a lot of surveillance cameras. They could already be on us if they caught the plane right after us and their tech is first rate."

"Baby, for this room, I used the MacAlister Visa card. We've never used it before. There's nothing to trace. Tomorrow morning we'll leave out by seven, cruise around until ten, make one last bank withdrawal, and then get as far away from any surveillance technology as we can while we wait on Billy to get back to us."

"I know it all sounds solid, but in the meantime I think we should be ready to run. Double-check the cameras in the other room."

"They're working."

"Humor me."

"Just a second." Janet put on a fresh bra. Then she took her laptop from the nightstand, sat on the bed, and opened the surveillance cameras that Allen had set up in the second-floor motel room that he'd rented with the Bixby credit card. "Doorway and room cameras working." She turned on the sound. "Air conditioner just kicked over."

"Okay. That's all we can hope for," Allen replied.

"Sleep in shifts?"

"I don't want to, but it's the smart play."

SEAN AND PHYLLIS sat in the Highlander in the side lot of an Exxon gasoline station across the street from the Holiday Inn Express.

"Terry knows his work," Phyllis said.

"Yes, he does. The Ford Focus is right there."

"So, catch them in the parking lot in the morning?"

Sean shook his head. "I've been thinking about this. I think the last three times we jumped the gun—didn't wait until we had the absolute most advantage. They're just too good to take under any normal circumstance. So now we're going to take our time, let them think they've escaped, and then tackle them when they think they're completely safe. Taking it slow is the quickest way to finally get this job done."

"Terry won't be any help if they stay away from cities and the interstate."

"No, he won't. And we can't be following too close, so we need to set a tracker. You go down the sidewalk where you can see if someone is coming out into the parking lot, and I'll put the tracker under the bumper."

Phyllis crossed the street and walked down the sidewalk toward the entrance to the Holiday Inn Express, acting as if she was looking at her phone. Sean walked into the parking lot as if he was going to his car. She texted him: *All clear.*

He dropped his car fob beside the Ford Focus and set the magnetic tracker under the bumper when he stooped to pick up the fob. Then he walked back across the street to the Highlander. Phyllis met him there.

She pulled up the tracker's app on her smartphone. "The signal's strong."

Sean nodded. "Nothing's probably going to happen before seven or eight o'clock, but we can't take that chance. You want to sleep first or second?"

"I'll sleep second."

"Okay." He reclined his seat. "Wake me up at three a.m."

6

At 1:45 a.m., Dido finally tracked the Bixbys to a Holiday Inn Express in Salt Lake City. She hacked into the hotel cameras and found their room on the second floor. She called Barney. "Where are you?"

"We're at a rest stop south of Salt Lake."

"They're at a Holiday Inn Express off of exit 294 A-C. Room 234."

"Gotcha."

"Remember, you've got to take them alive and get them to return Singh's money."

"We'll do our best."

At 2:15 A.M., Phyllis watched a green Nissan Pathfinder pull into the parking lot of the Holiday Inn Express and slowly drive through the entire lot before parking in a handicap space outside the swimming pool fence. Two people got out, a man and a woman wearing dark clothes and long raincoats. She shook Sean's arm. "Wake up. Something's up."

Sean rubbed his eyes. "What?"

Phyllis pointed. "There're two folks entering the motel from the swimming pool door."

"I see them. What're the chances that they're after someone other than our grifters?"

"They might save us some trouble."

"They might, but I doubt it. If the grifters were that easy to kill, they'd already be dead."

BARNEY AND ROBIN, dark clothes, Kevlar vests, and ballcaps, picked the lock on the door from the outside swimming pool to the first-floor hallway and crept up the stairwell to the second floor. Barney held a Mossberg pump-action shotgun down along his leg, and Robin carried an AR-15 rifle modified for automatic fire across her chest. The second-floor hall was empty. They tiptoed down the carpet, counting off the room numbers until they reached 234. They turned to look at each other and nodded. Barney shot through the door lock and kicked in the door. Robin stepped into the room and flipped on the lights. The room was empty. She pushed open the bathroom door, her rifle at the ready. No one. Barney looked in the closet. No clothes. No luggage.

"That was their car in the parking lot," Robin said.

"They're in the building, just not this room. The intel was bad," Barney said.

"Let's get out of here."

ALLEN HEARD the shotgun blast on the MacBook Air, looked on the laptop, and saw two people, a man and a woman, moving around the second-floor motel room. He shook Janet's shoulder. "Time to move."

They grabbed their guns, ran down the hall to the stairwell by the elevator, rushed down the steps two at a time, and positioned themselves against the wall at the front of the building between the front entrance and the swimming pool. When they heard footsteps coming from the doors to the swimming pool, they took cover behind some nearby cars and waited.

Two shadowy figures came through the chain-link gate from the swimming pool. Allen shot the first one in the legs. That figure went down. The other figure turned and fired a shotgun. Janet fired at his head and grazed his neck. He pumped his shotgun and pivoted toward her. She shot him in the chest. He staggered back and then fired. Janet ducked behind a pickup truck. "Vest," she yelled.

Allen popped up from behind a car and shot him in the face. He fell straight back, his head bouncing on the pavement. Janet ran toward the other figure, a woman who was pushing herself into a sitting position. Janet pulled the trigger on her Glock, but nothing happened. The woman swung her rifle around. Janet threw the pistol at her. It bounced off her chest. Janet dove behind a car as the woman fired a short burst. Allen swung around from behind a tire on a truck on the other side of the woman, fired twice, and hit her in the chest and head. She fell over sideways.

Janet stood up from behind the car.

"You okay?" Allen asked.

"Yeah." She picked up her Glock. "You?"

"Got nicked by a rifle round."

"How bad?"

"Not bad. Flesh wound, I think. Let's grab our bags and get out of here."

People were coming out into the hall or peeking out their doors as Allen and Janet rolled their bags down the hall to the stairwell. They lugged the bags down the steps, pushed through the exit door to the pool, and cut across the parking lot at a fast walk. Allen pressed the fob to open the trunk as they approached their car. They tossed their bags in, climbed into the front seats, and drove out of the parking lot.

"Pharmacy or medical supply?" Janet asked.

"Pharmacy."

"You sure?"

"I'm driving, aren't I?"

Janet opened Google on her phone. "There's a twenty-four-hour

CVS nearby. Ought to be able to get bandages and first aid stuff there. Let me set a route."

They drove in silence, listening to the app give directions, keeping an eye in their rearview mirror.

"No one's behind us," Allen said

"Those were new players," Janet said.

"Yeah. Sloppy and careless."

"They almost got lucky."

"We need better guns."

Allen drove into the CVS parking lot and parked away from the building. There were only three other cars in the lot. The early morning was quiet, the darkness slowly thinning away.

Janet turned on the flashlight on her smartphone. "Let me have a look."

Allen unbuttoned his shirt and turned in his seat. Janet used two fingers to move his shirt out of the way. "Not bleeding much. Ugly bruise. I'll get some antiseptic and a box of bandages."

She went into the CVS, found what she needed in the first aid section, and paid at the self-checkout. As she came back to the car, Allen got out. She set the bag of supplies on the trunk lid. "Lift up your shirt."

He held up his shirt. She sprayed antiseptic on the wound, placed a gauze square over it, and wrapped around his abdomen with a roll of gauze. "Really minor," she said. "Ought to quit bleeding on its own."

"Then why all the gauze?"

"Didn't want one of those big Band-Aids to come unstuck."

"Hurts like hell."

"I'm driving. You rest up."

Allen got in the passenger's side and reclined the seat. "Guess we're going to skip the bank run tomorrow."

Janet pulled a map up on her phone. "We're going to get on I-80 headed west, then get off on highway 93 heading south."

"Where does that lead?"

"To nowhere. Looks like we'll make it to a mom-and-pop motel with a gas station sometime in the morning."

"Good. Tomorrow we need to contact Billy and line up a full set of gear. Set a rendezvous where we can take possession."

Janet left the CVS parking lot, turned left and then right, heading for Interstate 15 North and Interstate 80 West.

THE CONTRACT KILLERS Sean and Phyllis pulled out of the Holiday Inn Express after the Ford Focus was out of sight, following the tracker signal.

"Don't let them get too far away," Phyllis said.

"I've got this figured out," Sean replied.

"They weren't playing around," Phyllis said.

"Nope. Those people were crazy going upstairs."

"Wonder if there is going to be more of them. If they keep stirring the pot, the grifters will never relax enough for us to ambush them."

"I'll bet you a steak dinner that those folks are done."

"Why so?"

"Not professionals."

"Which makes them unpredictable. I'll take that bet."

"It's going to cost you."

"We'll see."

THIRTY MINUTES LATER, Dido picked up information about a gunfight at the Holiday Inn Express on the Salt Lake City police scanner. She called Barney's phone number, but he didn't answer. She hacked the Holiday Inn surveillance cameras and spotted their Pathfinder parked next to the swimming pool, which meant they hadn't left. By 8:00 a.m., she'd found out there were two dead at the scene, both of whose descriptions matched Barney and Robin. She called Benny Singh's second in command, Olivia Blevins.

"Good news?"

"Barney and Robin are dead. The targets got away."

"How?"

"I wasn't there. Shootout at a Holiday Inn Express in Salt Lake City."

"Cops gotten in touch yet?"

"No."

"Keep me up to date."

"Of course."

OLIVIA BLEVINS PUT her phone in her dress pocket and opened a Salt Lake City news feed on her laptop computer. The headline read, "Organized Crime killings?" She scanned the article. What a clusterfuck. She got up from her desk. Better tell Benny. She walked across the hall to Singh's outer office and spoke to his personal assistant. "Jay, is Benny in?"

He nodded. "Just got here. Go on in."

Singh looked up from his laptop computer. "Olivia, what's up?"

She closed his office door. "Just heard from Dido."

"And?"

She walked up close to his desk and spoke softly. "Barney and Robin are dead. The targets got away."

"This can't be happening."

"What do you want to do?"

"I don't know."

"Do you want Dido to keep tracking them while you decide?"

"With a police investigation underway? We don't want the cops to find Dido doing anything that could raise more questions."

"Once we lose the grifters, it will be like starting from scratch."

"Don't care. We can't risk being discovered."

"I'll let her know."

SINGH WATCHED Olivia leave his office. It was clear that he wasn't going to be able to solve his money problems quickly. Olivia would wait until next month for her cut, and he could pay the minimum amounts on his credit cards. If he could stall the bank examiner, and if he used his line of credit, he'd be able to pay his child support and the rest of his monthly bills. He took a burner phone from his desk drawer and called Carl Thompson.

"Hello?"

"Carl, this is Benny. Can you talk? I've got some bad news."

"Give me a second to walk out into the parking lot." The line was quiet for a few minutes. "Okay, I can talk."

"Someone broke into my personal mutual fund account and cleaned out my cash."

"What? How?"

"We're trying to figure it out. There's no easy way to say this, but you're going to have to wait for next month to be paid."

"I can't wait. I need that money."

"Well, I don't have it. I'll make a double payment next month. That's the best I can do."

"That's not good enough."

"You're not the only one in a bind. Olivia's waiting. I can't pay my own bills."

"You've got to find another way."

"I can't."

"To hell with you." Thompson ended the call.

Singh put away his burner phone. Carl could curse all he wanted to. There was nothing he could do to pressure him. They both knew it. He might be pissed off, but he was just going to have to wait.

CARL THOMPSON PUT his Singh burner phone into his back pocket and took out his Travelers phone. It ran four times before the man answered.

"I thought I told you not to call."

"I've heard from Singh that you scored. I'm expecting my money."

"We've been a little busy, but we'll transfer the cash today."

"When?"

"We'll start the process within the hour. The $10,000 will drop into your account from a numbered account in the Caymans within two days."

"Why so long?"

"So it's scrubbed clean when you get it."

"I'll be waiting."

ALLEN PUT his bank examiner phone away. He and Janet were sitting in the diner attached to the Jericho Motel on alternate highway 93 in Eastern Nevada. The landscape was like a movie set from an old western, wide canyons and tall cliffs, except for the power poles following the highway. They were drinking their second cups of coffee, empty breakfast dishes in front of them. "You hear all that?"

She nodded. "I can set up the transfer when we get back to our room."

"I'll be happy to be done with him."

"Me too." She glanced at an old man pushing through the front door. "So who do you think the new team was? They weren't good enough to be with Orange Hill."

"I don't know. Singh could have hired them. Could have been from Elemental Security. And you're right, Sean and Phyllis could run rings around them."

"We should change cars again."

"We should, but we don't want to go anywhere where we might get picked up on a surveillance camera. So let's wait a little bit, make sure we've lost Sean and Phyllis, and get properly geared up."

Janet pulled up a map app on her phone. "South of us is Ely. Small town with a lot of motels. We could collect our gear there."

"Good idea. Lots of tourists in a town like that. We just need to stay away from the motels."

"We could pick up our gear at a park or something and keep driving."

"It's a plan."

They paid their bill at the cash register and went outside, where they walked away from the doors but stayed under the awning. Allen took out his phone and called Billy.

"How did that equipment work out for you?"

"Better than nothing, but we need a full set a gear—vests, rifles, handguns, magnetic trackers, and smoke grenades if you can get them."

"Where can you take delivery?"

"Ely, Nevada."

"Okay, give me a second." The phone was quiet for a few minutes. "I can get the gear there in two days."

"That'll work."

"On the day of, I'll have the final details."

"Thanks, Billy."

Allen filled in Janet.

Janet opened her map app. "It's only about an hour or so to Ely, so if we stay here overnight, switch from alternate 93 to regular 93 and head north before we circle back around, we could take two days to get to Ely. It'll give you time to heal up."

"And we can move most of the money from the Provo bank to the Portland bank."

"Let's wash it through the Denver bank first. Then no one can track it without a court order."

"Agreed," Allen said. "After we use the internet in our room to pay Thompson and move our money, no internet and no cell phones until we have our gear."

"The longer we circle around in the desert, the better our chances are of losing Sean and Phyllis. Once we get rid of them, we'll be able to focus on getting Orange Hill off our backs."

"If Billy can find us a score."

SEAN AND PHYLLIS sat in their Highlander on the side of the road north of the Jericho Motel. Phyllis looked at the tracker app on her phone. "They haven't moved in an hour and a half."

"Maybe they've stopped for the day."

"Maybe."

"Maybe they're resting up after driving since 3:30 a.m."

"They don't know this car. Let's do a drive-by. Fill up our gas tank if it looks safe."

They drove over the hill and down to the motel. The gas pumps sat in front of the restaurant.

"There's the Ford Focus," Phyllis said. "Sitting in front of room 16. We're in the middle of nowhere. No cops, only a few witnesses. If we move fast, we could take them here and be gone."

"We've been over this," Sean replied. "We're not going to get in a hurry. That's how we missed them before. Every time we attempt to take them, we're also at risk. We could get killed just as easily as them. You saw what they did last night. I want the odds tilted so far that we can't lose. And that's not a broad daylight attempt on a first-floor motel room. Not when we've got a tracker on their car."

"Fair enough."

"We're going to wait for them to box themselves in, and then we're going to take advantage."

DIDO'S LANDLINE PHONE RANG. "Elemental Security."

"This is Sergeant Fuentes with the Salt Lake City Police."

"How can I help you?"

"Do you know Barney Roman and Robin Sikes?"

"Yes. What's up?"

"Are they employed by Elemental Security?"

"They're freelance. They do work for us from time-to-time."

"Are they working on a case for you right now?"

"No. What's the problem? Have they been arrested?"

"There's no easy way to say this, ma'am. They're dead."

"Dead? That's impossible."

"They were killed in a fire fight at a Holiday Inn Express early this morning."

"My God. Were there any witnesses? Do you have any leads?"

"We're talking with anyone who might know something, which is why I called you."

"I wish I could help."

"Do you have their personal information?"

"They were both single. Lived alone."

"No relatives?"

"None that I know of."

"Thank you for your time."

Dido called Olivia Blevins on her cell phone. "Cops just called about Barney and Robin."

"And?"

"They don't know anything. I told them Barney and Robin were freelance and not currently working for us."

"Thanks, Dido."

7

The next morning, Allen and Janet drove south until they came to highway 93, turned north, and then circled west and south through a tiny town called Ruby Valley and back north on highway 228 to Elko, Nevada. "We're getting low on gas," Janet said.

"This town is too big to stop in. It'll have plenty of surveillance cameras."

"There's a small town where we get off Interstate 80 and head south on highway 278."

"Population?"

"A little over two thousand."

"We'll stop there."

After they bought gas and got packaged sandwiches, chips, and bottled iced tea from the convenience store on the outskirts of Carlin, Nevada, they headed south on highway 278, where they spent the night at Rooster Dan's Provision Company, eight small motel rooms and a tiny grocery store.

The next day they got on highway 50 at Eureka and drove east to Ely.

"Pretty country," Allen said.

"We've made the circle."

"And we've stayed off the grid. Text Billy."

Janet texted Billy. A few minutes later she got a reply, which she read to Allen.

Silver Ford F-150 crew cab parked in the outer lot to the south of the Love's Travel Stop. Nearby surveillance camera is broken. Key fob pushed under passenger's side front tire. You can take the truck or just the gear in the back seat.

They drove into Ely on highway 50, paying attention to the speed limit, and turned onto Great Basin Boulevard. "Love's is up on the right," Janet said.

Allen pulled into the parking lot, drove around to the back of the building, through the overnight parking area to the outer perimeter. A silver F-150 sat under a light pole with a surveillance camera peering down. Allen pulled up next to the driver's side.

Janet hopped out of the Ford Focus, jogged around to the passenger's side of the F-150, and found the key fob tucked under the front tire. She held the fob up for Allen to see. He got out of the car.

"Should we switch vehicles?" she asked.

"The car's been on surveillance cameras, but nobody knows the truck. Let's have a look."

She pressed the button on the fob. Allen opened the driver's door and glanced around the interior. Two large duffels sat in the back seat floorboard. He popped the hood, went around to the front of the truck, lifted the hood, and looked at the engine.

"What do you think?" she asked.

"Nothing leaking. Let's hear how it sounds."

Allen got in the truck, started it, and drove around the parking lot while Janet waited by the Ford Focus. He parked on the other side of the car, turned off the truck, and got out. "Let's keep the truck."

They moved their roller bags into the back seat of the truck and then wiped down the interior of the Ford Focus. Allen wiped off the car's key fob and tossed it onto the floorboard.

"We forget anything?"

Janet shook her head. "Should we check the duffels?"

"Let's do that somewhere else. Don't want to press our luck."

"Continue down US 93?"

"Yeah, we can switch up before we get to Las Vegas."

SEAN AND PHYLLIS were sitting in the Highlander in the parking lot of a Rolberto's Mexican Restaurant on Great Basin Boulevard. Phyllis was looking at the tracker app on her phone. "They're still at the Love's Travel Stop."

"They haven't moved in almost an hour."

"Eating lunch? Gassing up?"

"This doesn't follow their MO," Sean said. "They haven't stopped at any big chains. We need to take a look."

They drove down to the Love's, drove slowly around the lot, looking for a red Ford Focus, until they finally spotted it in the farthest parking lot from the building. No one was in it. They pulled up beside it. Phyllis climbed out and looked in the driver's window, taking care not to touch anything. She glanced over her shoulder. "It's been cleaned out."

"Damn it," Sean said. "Pull the tracker and let's get out of here."

Phyllis removed the tracker from under the rear bumper and got back into the SUV. "What's the hurry? We're starting from scratch. We don't know what they're driving. We might as well go back to that Mexican restaurant and have lunch."

"Go ahead and say it if you want to."

"I told you so? Could have taken them at the motel? Why? Your reasoning made good sense at the time. This was the risk."

"Yeah, just didn't expect them to get so lucky. They never found the tracker."

"Think so?"

"They would have dumped it a long time ago if they'd known it was there."

"So they switched vehicles for another reason," Phyllis said. "Why? Did they meet friends? Pick up supplies? Were they going to switch all along?"

"We may never find out. Call Terry and get him checking the public surveillance cameras circling out from here."

ALLEN AND JANET drove into Pioche, Nevada, on Main Street and stopped at the Sinclair gas station. One employee sat at the counter inside. There were no other cars at the pumps. After Allen filled the tank, they drove around the side of the building to have a look at the gear Billy had sent them. They opened the crew cab doors, set their luggage out on the pavement, and pulled the duffels up onto the seats. Phyllis opened the one on the right. Two Glock pistols, three full magazines, two boxes of shells, a box of four magnetic trackers, and a box containing four smoke bombs. Allen opened the one on the left. Two AR-15 rifles, full magazines and extra shells, two Kevlar vests, night vision goggles, and a Taser.

"All top quality," Allen said.

"Billy is always reliable."

"Great guy to work with, no doubt."

They continued down Main Street to the Historic Silver Café and stopped to eat. While they were drinking coffee after their meal, Allen got a call from Billy.

"How's the truck?"

"Thanks for your help. All the equipment looks good."

"I've got the info you want."

"We're in a restaurant. Give us a few minutes to get to the truck and I'll put you on speaker."

They paid the check and went out to the F-150, where they called Billy back.

"Like I said, I found your job, but you're not going to like it."

"Keep talking."

"Mr. Wishes has three ongoing operations that probably produce most of his income: gambling, gun smuggling and human trafficking, and drug smuggling. My sources say the gambling is strictly his, while he takes a cut of the other two for facilitating transfer across the Mexican border."

"So disrupting the gun smuggling and human trafficking, as well as the drug smuggling, would get him into trouble with Orange Hill?"

"They wouldn't be happy."

"What details do you have about the gambling operation?"

"It's in a private residence near the airport in Jackson, Wyoming. It's strictly card games. They have hostesses and a full bar."

"Okay. What about the gun smuggling and human trafficking?"

"Semitrucks going through El Paso. A guy tells me the cover is Manning Brothers Freight Company moving construction materials, but it's really guns into Mexico and sex workers into the US."

"And the drug smuggling?"

"Fentanyl coming across the Arizona desert."

"Thanks, Billy."

"What are you going to do?"

"We'll be in touch." He ended the call.

"Garcia won't be interested in the gambling," Janet said.

"No, but it would be fun to poke Mr. Wishes in the eye, and we could use the money to finance the other two jobs, which won't be profitable at all unless we stumble over a stash."

"So you want to do them all?"

"I want Mr. Wishes discredited and afraid for his life, broke and looking over his shoulder."

"This is going to be crazy hard."

"Harder than breaking me out of jail?"

"Three different places? We don't know the lay of the land."

"So let's go up to Jackson, Wyoming, and check things out. If it's not doable, we'll move on. I just don't want to leave any low-hanging fruit."

"Okay, let's take a look."

"Find a route that keeps us away from as many cameras as possible."

They spent the night sleeping at a gravel parking lot along a river in southwestern Wyoming. At dawn, they stopped at Cousin's Coffee Mill and ate breakfast with a roomful of tourists planning their day's fishing. They continued north on US Highway 189, stopping for gas and sandwiches, merged onto US-191, and arrived in Jackson Hole before dark.

"How much farther to Jackson?"

"Just up the valley."

"Keep you eyes open for a rundown motel without surveillance cameras."

They pulled into the Wagon Wheel Motel, a strip of rooms anchored by a two-pump gas station/convenience store that was set into the woods on the side of the road. Two semitrucks were parked on the far side of the gas pumps. Janet put on a blonde wig and a sweatshirt before she went into the convenience store.

A big-built woman in a track suit and ponytail sat on a stool behind the cash register. "Can I help you?"

"I'm looking for a room."

"How many days?"

"Three or four. Depends on what we get up to."

Janet paid for three days in cash and took the keycard. They rolled their bags into the room. Cigarette burns on the bedside tables, thin towels, and a rust-stained shower. The back window looked out on a junk car on blocks. "We can sure pick them," Janet said.

"Nobody's going to find us here," Allen said.

They drove north into Jackson and continued on US-191 through town. "These western tourist towns are all pretty much the same," Janet said. "Cowboy bars, coffee shops, historical landmarks, gift shops."

"Yeah," Allen said, "but you've got to admit this is a pretty nice version."

"Didn't say it wasn't."

They drove up into an upscale residential neighborhood near the airport. The houses stood on one acre lots with fencing at the lot lines. "The gambling operation is supposed to be in this neighborhood."

They drove past several houses that appeared to be empty, while others had one or two cars in the driveway and a few lights on. Down a cul-de-sac, they saw a gigantic mountain stone home at the end of a long driveway. Security lights shined down all around the perimeter of the house. Allen stopped their truck.

"How many cars parked in front of the garage?"

Janet counted. "Ten."

"There's a surveillance camera on the gable end of the garage," Allen said.

"They don't hide them anymore, do they?"

Allen lowered his window and whistled as loud as he could. Two large, black dogs appeared from around the side of the house and started running toward the gate on the driveway.

"This could be the place. Can you get a picture of the cars?"

"Colors and shapes. It's too far for the license plates." She took three photos with her phone.

"Let's drive back out to the highway. Find a place to park. See how late these visitors stay out."

They drove back down to US 191 and pulled off at a farm gate with a good view of the street into the subdivision.

"Not much to hide behind here," Janet said.

"They won't be looking for us, at least not this time."

The first vehicle, a white Toyota Highlander, came out of the subdivision and drove toward town at 11:35 p.m. Over the next fifteen minutes, seven other vehicles left, some going north and some going south.

"So the game breaks up around 11:30," Janet said.

"Let's come back tomorrow at 11:00 p.m. If everyone leaves around 11:30, maybe we'll be able to reconnoiter the house, find out if it's the one we're looking for."

"And go ahead and break in."

"I like the way you think."

When they parked in front of their motel room at the Wagon Wheel Motel, they noticed the door was ajar. Allen and Janet both hopped out of their truck with their Glocks in their hands. Allen scanned the parking lot and looked over toward the gas pumps. There was no one in sight. Janet crept up to the door and pushed it open. Then she reached inside and turned on the overhead light.

Their roller bags lay open on the bed. Janet stepped across the room to the bathroom, holding her pistol in both hands. The bathroom was empty. Allen went to his bag and looked through the contents. "Everything's here, I think."

Janet checked her bag. "Me, as well."

Allen chuckled. "So someone came to rob us and didn't find anything they liked."

"Good thing we took our gear with us."

"Leave or stay?"

"We want our footprint to be as small as possible," Janet said. "As long as we don't leave anything here, we ought to be okay."

"Let's pull our gear out of the truck, just in case someone breaks in overnight."

In the morning, they went down to the convenience store for coffee. The big-boned woman with the ponytail was sitting on the stool behind the cash register as if she'd never left.

"How did you sleep?" she asked.

"Someone broke into our room while we were out," Janet said.

"Really? I'm sorry to hear that."

"Any extra keycards floating around?" Allen asked.

"Not that I know of. You missing anything?"

"No," Janet said, "I guess we don't have anything worth stealing."

"Where's the creamer?" Allen asked.

"At the end of the counter." She pointed down the counter to bowls containing packets of sugar and non-dairy creamer. Allen put creamer in his coffee.

"You guys going hiking today? Or you doing something in town?"

"I think we'll figure it out at breakfast."

"It's clear today, but it's going to be rain tomorrow."

They went back down to their room and moved their gear and roller bags out to their truck. Then Allen put a scrap of paper in the doorjamb, and they drove off toward town.

"Did you believe her?"

"About the weather forecast? Yes. About the break-in? She was too nonchalant. It either happens all the time, or she knows who's doing it and they split whatever they steal."

"At least they didn't steal my new underwear," Janet replied.

"Probably the wrong size."

They spent the day driving around in Grand Teton National Park and then went up to Yellowstone National Park to see the Old Faithful geyser, but they didn't get out of the truck. "Lots of people," Janet said.

"Let's find a place to eat dinner and then rest up for tonight."

"What do you want to eat?"

"Don't care."

"Take-out pizza?"

"Fine by me."

They went back to their motel room to eat their pizza and rest up for the evening. They left their gear and their luggage in the truck. If they robbed the party house tonight, they wouldn't be coming back.

8

At 10:30 p.m., Allen and Janet were sitting in their truck on the side of the street at the base of the cul-de-sac. They were wearing dark-colored clothes. The vehicles started coming out from the cul-de-sac at 11:15. They waited until 12:30 a.m. Then they drove into the cul-de-sac and parked next to the ditch on the outside of the fence surrounding the party house. There were no cars in the driveway, and only two lights on in the front of the house.

"It's dead," Janet said. "Want to take a look?"

"Yeah, let's have a look. If it's the party house and no one is there, we can go ahead and do the job."

Allen disabled the interior light in the truck, and they got out, taking care to ease the doors shut. Allen was carrying a small backpack of tools. He handed Janet the Taser. "For the dogs."

They jogged up the lawn to the left of the driveway, keeping in the shadows near a bank of bushes. When they got to the house, they put on throwaway gloves and put their hoods up before they crept to the nearest window and peeked in. An empty dining room with a view of the living room beyond. One of the dogs walked through the living room.

Allen and Janet snuck around to the side of the garage. "Dogs are inside, which is tricky," Allen said.

At the back of the house, light was shining out from an egress window. Allen leaned over to look inside. The basement had been remodeled into a gambling room—carpeted floor, card tables, and a wet bar with stools at the far end. He whispered to Janet, "This is definitely the right place."

They heard the garage door opening and scurried around the building to see two people leaving in a Porsche.

"So it's just us and the dogs," Allen said.

"Think the safe is in the basement?"

"That would make sense, wouldn't it? I don't want to Tase the dogs, but we won't have any choice if we can't shut them in a room we don't need."

"Okay, where do you think the alarm panel is?"

"Front door and garage?"

"If we trip the alarm, we won't get another chance to rob this place."

"That was always the case."

They walked around the garage side door. The electric meter and breaker box hung on the wall next to it. "The weakest link is the padlock on the breaker box," Janet said.

"An alarm system on a stash house has got to have battery backup." Allen took a palm-size box with a display on one side and two wires with clip ends hanging from the bottom and pressed the "on" button to make sure it worked. "Password breaker is good to go." He turned to Janet. "You ready?"

She nodded.

He handed her the password breaker. Then he took his lockpick set out of the backpack, inserted the tension wrench in the bottom of the keyhole, applied slight pressure in the direction that he would turn the key, and then scrubbed his lock pick across the pins in the top of the keyhole until the pins fell into place, and he could turn the tension wrench, unlocking the door. He put his lockpick set back in the backpack. "Hand me the password breaker."

Janet handed him the device and a flat blade screwdriver. He opened the garage side door, turned on the lights, and saw the alarm panel next to the backdoor. He rushed across the garage, used the screwdriver to pop the cover off the alarm panel, clipped two wires from the password breaker onto the circuit board of the alarm panel, and switched it on. He had forty-five seconds before the alarm sounded.

The display on the password breaker showed numbers flashing by as the device found the password number by number. Thirty seconds. Two numbers left. Twenty seconds. One number left. Ten seconds. The last number came up and the red light on the alarm turned off. Allen turned the handle on the door to the kitchen. It was unlocked. He could hear the dogs sniffing and pawing. He waved Janet over. "Keep the dogs here," he whispered.

Allen hurried back around the house to the egress window, climbed down into the window well, and looked into the basement gambling room. All clear. He forced a pry bar under the bottom edge of the double-hung window and applied slow, even pressure, taking care to be as quiet as possible. The window lock popped free. He raised the window a few inches and listened. He could hear both dogs barking at the garage door. He slid the window the rest of the way up and climbed inside. He glanced up at the open door at the top of the stairs and hurried across the room. As he reached the first step, someone grabbed his collar and threw him down on the floor. A big man, shaved head and braided beard, stood over him holding a pistol. "Hector! Ajax!" he called.

The dogs came running. The man motioned at Allen with his gun. "On your feet."

Allen got up. The dogs bounded down the steps and circled him, growling and nipping at his legs. He had his hands up.

"Who are you and why are you here?" the man said. "Don't make me set the dogs on you."

"I'm Bryce Cotter," Allen said. "Cotter Security. I was hired to test the security system here."

"That's bullshit."

"My card is in my wallet."

"Why wasn't I told?"

"It wouldn't be a test if you knew it was coming, would it?"

MEANWHILE, Janet stood at the top of the stairs, Taser in her right hand and her pistol tucked into her pants at her waist.

"Take out your wallet," Braided Beard said to Allen.

Allen reached into his back pocket and brought out his wallet.

"Hand it here."

Allen held the wallet out at the end of his arm. Braided Beard snatched it and stepped back. The dogs kept circling and growling. While Braided Beard was opening the wallet, Janet crept down two steps to get within Taser range and fired her Taser. Braided Beard swiveled toward her as the darts struck him. He shuddered and fell over. The dogs looked up at Janet. She dropped the Taser and yelled. They started up the stairs. She ran for the garage door. Allen rushed up the steps and shut the door to the basement. When he turned, Braided Beard was on his hands and knees, shaking his head. Allen ran down the stairs and kicked him in the face. He collapsed to the floor. Allen took a length of rope from his backpack and tied Braided Beard's wrists to his ankles. Then he trotted up the stairs and banged his fist on the door. He heard the dogs rushing back across the first floor. They barked and clawed at the door. He went back down into the basement gambling room and picked up his wallet.

He was looking behind an art print hanging on the wall at the bottom of the stairs when Janet climbed in from the egress window. "Find anything?"

"Nothing yet," Allen said.

"We need to keep moving," Janet said. "I've got a feeling there's a quiet alarm we didn't find."

"You start on the right. I'll continue over here."

They moved through the room, opening cabinets and looking behind pictures to find a hidden wall safe. They finally ended up behind the bar. Allen pulled aside a rubber floor mat. "Over here."

Janet joined him. A floor safe with a combination dial was built into the concrete floor. "What do you think?"

"I'm going to crack it old school."

"You better hurry."

Allen got down on his knees, opened his backpack, and took out a pencil, a piece of graph paper, and a pocket-size book containing combination sequences for various brands of safes. He looked up the brand of safe. Three numbers. Right, left, and right. He tried the factory set combination. No luck. He put the book away and spun the combination dial to the right. Starting at zero, he slowly turned the dial to the left, listening for the click that indicated a possible combination number, and wrote it on the paper. Then he started over, three numbers to the left of zero, listening once again for the subtle click that indicated a possible combination number.

"You need to move faster," Janet said.

"You can't rush it. Go stand in the driveway and watch if you're worried about company."

After about ten minutes, through trial and error, he'd graphed out the three combination numbers. But which order? He worked his way through the various combinations until the safe opened on the fifth try.

"I was beginning to think you lost your touch," Janet said.

"Don't get to go old school very often anymore. But in this case, we don't want any marks on the safe. We want Mr. Wishes to know it's us."

He lifted the lid and pulled out three cloth bags, each with a tag indicating the date the cash was collected.

Janet took the bags to a table and dumped them out.

"What have we got?"

"If the notes are correct, it's $125,000."

He closed the safe and spun the dial. "Let's get out of here."

"What about him?" She nodded toward Braided Beard, still out cold.

"He's going to provide our descriptions. I'd love to be here to see Mr. Wishes' face. He's going to go crazy."

They climbed out the egress window and shut it. As they were moving across the lawn, keeping to the bushes away from the driveway, the Porsche slid through the turn from the cul-de-sac to the driveway and powered up to the garage, where it skidded to a halt. Three men rushed up the sidewalk to the front door, pistols in their hands.

As soon as the door closed behind the men, Allen and Janet tore off down the lawn, scrambled over the fence, and climbed into their truck. Allen drove two blocks before he turned on the headlights. He got back onto US-191 headed south into Jackson. The town was quiet. No one seemed to be following them.

"Go back south the way we came?" Janet asked.

"It's the surest way. But we should probably break our pattern at Salt Lake."

"Okay, I'll chart a route from Salt Lake to El Paso." She chuckled.

"What?"

"You should have seen the look on your face while you were trying to con that bro."

"Was it off?"

"No, you had complete sincerity going on. He was almost buying it."

"He was a big boy. I wasn't going to be able to surprise him when he grabbed my wallet."

"Well, you didn't have to, did you?"

"You were wearing your superhero cape. Handled the dogs like a dog whisperer."

"Dogs love me."

"Those dogs would have loved to bite you."

"Maybe." She patted his thigh. "$125,000 isn't so much money."

"Yeah, I wish it had been more. But the important thing is that we're teaching him that we can disrupt his business. He's going to find out that we can play this game just as well as he can."

. . .

TWO DAYS LATER, Mr. Wishes landed at the Jackson Hole airport. He came off the plane carrying an overnight bag, a scowling pale-skinned man in a dark suit. Two people were waiting for him—a middle-age blonde wearing outdoorsy clothes and a young man wearing jeans and a cargo jacket.

"Geraldine," Mr. Wishes said. He shook her hand. Then he handed his bag to the young man. "Who is he?"

"Craig? He's your driver. He's one of the new ones."

Mr. Wishes nodded his head. "Let's not waste my time."

They got into a Hyundai Tucson SUV, Craig driving, came out of the airport and drove immediately into the nearby neighborhood. A few minutes later, they pulled up to the garage of a sprawling mountain stone house on an acreage. Everyone got out of the SUV. Mr. Wishes turned to Craig. "Stay here."

"Yes, sir." Craig got back into the SUV.

Mr. Wishes and Geraldine went up to the door. "He knows what's going on here," Geraldine said.

"He hasn't heard me say anything or seen me do anything."

Two men met them in the living room. "Where is he?"

"Big Jim is watching him downstairs."

Mr. Wishes and Geraldine went downstairs to the basement party room. Among the card tables, the big guy with the braided beard was duct-taped into a chair, his arms and legs double-wrapped. His face was a mass of purple bruises and bleeding cuts. An enormous man with a cauliflower ear and a crushed eye orbit stood in front of him, brass knuckles on his right hand, drinking from a can of beer.

"Big Jim," Geraldine said.

The enormous man turned, saw Mr. Wishes, and stepped to the side.

"Find out anything?"

Big Jim shook his head.

Mr. Wishes dragged over a chair from a nearby table, placed it directly in front of Braided Beard, and sat down. "Timmy, Timmy, Timmy. You know how this looks, right? It looks like your friends didn't do a good enough job of making this look like a robbery. It looks like you let them in. It's hard to believe that anyone got by you and the dogs and didn't get torn up at least a little bit."

Timmy sat there looking down.

"You can talk."

"Mr. Wishes, I know how it sounds. But it happened just like I said."

Big Jim stepped over to smack him. Mr. Wishes raised his hand and shook his head.

"Okay, Timmy, you tell me what happened. Don't leave anything out."

He nodded and drew in a deep breath. "It was my turn to spend the night. We draw straws so no one knows if they're the one who's staying. After Digger and KC left, I was walking around the perimeter, making sure all the doors and windows were locked. The dogs were a little antsy, but everything was locked down tight. I set the perimeter alarm. I went into the kitchen to make a sandwich, the dogs were following me, but then they took off to the garage door and started barking.

"I thought the dogs had that covered, so I went downstairs, got out my Glock, and stood in the dead zone where no one can see you through the windows. A guy came in through the window over there." He nodded toward the egress window to his left. "I called the dogs. That's where I made my mistake. A woman Tased me from the top of the stairs. The dogs went after her. The guy kicked me in the head. When I woke up, I was trussed up and Digger and KC were standing over me."

"It's like I was saying, boss," Geraldine added, "either all of them were in it together or Timmy's telling the truth."

"Did the two robbers call each other by name?"

"No, sir."

"What did the guy look like?"

"About six feet, regular looking, nothing distinctive."

"And the woman?"

"Even wearing hiking clothes, she was a knock-out."

"That pretty?"

"Like a movie star."

Mr. Wishes went to the floor safe behind the bar. "Who has the combination?"

"I do," Geraldine said. "I make change during the game."

"Why aren't you taped in this chair?"

"I wasn't here. Timmy, Digger, and KC all saw me close the safe."

"And if I dig into you, I'm not going to find you've been meeting with the robbers?"

"No, sir."

Mr. Wishes got down on his knees and turned on the flashlight on his phone. There were no marks or scratches on the door to the safe. Someone opened it without using tools. A man and a woman. They overrode the alarm. Dealt with Timmy and the dogs. Opened the safe lickety-split. It couldn't be. The grifters wouldn't dare come after him. But it had to be them. This was exactly how they worked.

He turned to Big Jim. "Cut him loose."

Big Jim cut through the duct tape with a lockback knife.

Mr. Wishes looked at Timmy. "Can you walk?"

"I can try."

Mr. Wishes took a wad of cash from his pocket, counted out $5,000, and shoved it in Timmy's shirt pocket. "Geraldine. Get the guys to come down here and take Timmy to our doctor."

Geraldine went upstairs.

"I'm sorry for the misunderstanding," Mr. Wishes said. "But you've proven yourself now. I'll talk to Geraldine about getting you a better job, one that rewards your honesty and loyalty."

Digger and KC came downstairs. Geraldine walked back outside with Mr. Wishes. "Are you spending the night?" she asked.

"Yes, but I won't need any companionship. Have you got a hacker?"

"Yes."

"Have them check all the surveillance feeds at gas stations, motels and rest stops. The robbers have got to be on a surveillance feed somewhere."

"Based on Timmy's description?"

"Yes."

"Some aren't accessible from the internet."

"Check all the ones that are."

"I'll put the hacker on it right away."

"And find a better job for Timmy. If he falls into place, great. If he's still skittish in a month, he might become unreliable. In which case, accident or drug overdose. Is he married?"

"No, sir."

"All the better."

"Are you staying at the condo in town?"

"Yes. Get the games back up and running. I'm going to go over the books. I'll check in with you tomorrow before I leave."

Mr. Wishes got into the back seat of the SUV.

Craig started it. "Where to?"

"The condo out by the ski lifts."

"Yes sir."

Mr. Wishes sat back in his seat. The grifters found his private game and robbed him while he was hunting them all over the US. Did they think he'd give up on them if they pushed back? They weren't that naïve. What was their game then? What were they up to?

He looked out the window at the chaparral flying by as they sped toward town. The contract killers, Sean and Phyllis, weren't getting the job done. They'd missed their chance three times. Who else could he get? There were maybe four other crews as good as they were. Two of them worked for competitors. One of them got caught up in an FBI sting. He hadn't been able to find the last one, maybe dead, maybe retired. Either way he was of no help to him. He needed to put the pressure on Sean and Phyllis. The grifters had been a problem for way too long.

Later that afternoon, he got a call from Geraldine. "Our hacker spotted several couples who might be the ones you're looking for."

"Email the footage."

She sent along five bits of video, all taken at various gas stations. Mr. Wishes opened them one by one. When he opened the third one, he saw the grifters. He was at the gas pump. She was leaning out of the driver's side window of a F-150 club cab pickup truck. God damn it. There they were, teasing him like they were the ones in control. He emailed the clip to Sean.

His message said: *Here they are in Jackson, Wyoming. Find them and eliminate them. Stop wasting my time.*

Sean read Mr. Wishes' email, Phyllis looking over his shoulder. "Jackson, Wyoming," Phyllis said. "How could Mr. Wishes have spotted them there?"

"Can't be good," Sean replied. "And you know they're not there anymore. Time stamp is a day old."

"But it is a place for Terry to start from."

9

Allen and Janet were driving between truck stops along Interstate 25 north of El Paso, looking for semitrucks painted with the Manning Brothers Freight logo. They found one parked around the side of the building at AJ's Travel Center.

"What do you think?" Allen asked.

"We need to test Billy's information," Janet replied.

"Agreed. We need to get a look in the trailer, find the hidden compartment, and see what's in there."

"Going south would be guns."

Allen nodded. "Going north should be people, which makes disrupting them all the sweeter. I hate slavers."

"Is Garcia going to care which it is?"

"I don't think so. As long as it's not toaster ovens."

"We need to move fast. We're bound to be on surveillance cameras at these truck stops."

They pulled into a car parking space where they could watch the Manning Brothers semitruck.

After dark, another Manning Brothers semitruck pulled up

beside the first one. The drivers got out of their trucks and went into the building together. Janet followed at a distance. The drivers went into the restaurant, sat at a table, and started reading menus. Janet called Allen. "They're eating dinner. You've got twenty minutes."

Allen picked the padlock on the trailer door of the first truck and swung one side open. Two by fours, two by sixes, windows in cardboard packing and shrink wrap, rolls of house wrap. He climbed up into the trailer, turned on his flashlight, and closed the door behind him. He slipped through the construction materials until he came to stacked bundles of roof shingles. He moved a few bundles so that he could continue to the front of the trailer. At the front wall, he put his ear to the wall and rapped on it with his knuckles. There was a space behind this wall. Not very wide, but a space none the less. Where was the door?

He held his flashlight near to the wall, moving his arm in a circle, hoping to see a vertical line, but he found nothing. He got a text from Janet. The truckdrivers were finished eating. He replaced the bundles of shingles on his way out, climbed out of the trailer, and replaced the lock. Janet met him back at their truck.

"Did you find anything?"

"There's definitely a hidden compartment at the front end of the trailer, but I couldn't find a way into it. I needed more time."

They watched the truck drivers get back into their trucks. The original semitruck drove out of the truck stop. Allen and Janet followed, watched the semitruck get onto the interstate headed toward the Mexican border, and then returned to the truck stop parking lot.

"That one had the guns," Janet said.

"More than likely," Allen replied. "But what's in the other one? Let's go back and wait."

Later, after the traffic slowed down and the last few trucks pulled into the truck stop to rest overnight, a Jeep pulled up next to the Manning Brothers semitruck. The driver got out of the truck and got into the Jeep. When he opened the door and the interior light came on, they saw that the driver was a brunette woman wearing an open flannel shirt over a T-shirt. The Jeep drove away.

"I'm going to say that was strictly against company policy," Allen said.

"How long do you think they'll be gone?"

"Long enough. Keep an eye out."

Allen walked across the parking lot, picked the padlock on the back door to the trailer, climbed inside, turned on his flashlight, and shut the door. The trailer was full of pre-hung interior doors, the boxes stacked together to leave a tiny aisle down the middle of the trailer. Allen walked down the aisle, stepping carefully to avoid making any unnecessary sound. At the front of the trailer, he got down on his hands and knees and crawled along the front wall. Near the corner, he found an inset latch to a two-foot by two-foot door. He pushed the door open. Bright light blinded him. When his eyes adjusted, he saw he was looking into a space about three feet wide that was crowded with young women lying on foam. They inched back away from him.

"English?"

A woman wearing jeans and a loose, white blouse raise her hand.

"What is your name?"

"Angelita."

"Please translate. You're in the US. Do you want to stay in this truck or leave?"

The woman spoke to the others in Spanish.

"We want to leave."

"Come on then."

He waited outside the trailer as the women trickled out. Some of them walked away by themselves, others stayed in groups. When Angelita climbed out, Allen took her by the arm. "I need your help a while longer. Then I'll help you get away from here."

"Why should I trust you?"

"I'm not going to harm you. But if you yell or make a scene, you'll end up arrested and deported."

He locked the back of the truck and led her by the arm to the F-

150. Janet lowered her window. Allen nodded toward her. "This is my wife, Janet."

"Pleased to meet you," Janet said.

Allen opened the back door, and Angelita got in. He walked around to the passenger's side.

Janet turned to him. "What's the deal?"

"Angelita is going to help us convince Garcia. Then we're going to help her get on her way."

Janet turned to Angelita. "Why were you in that truck?"

"I had to come here to the US to work or my little brother was going to have to join the gang."

"That's worse?"

"My mom needs my brother to work, or she'll lose her apartment."

"So you came to the US to be a sex worker?"

She looked down at the floorboard. "The coyotes have already used me. It's not so bad if they don't hit you."

"You think they won't take your brother anyway?"

"This was our only chance."

"What are you going to do now?"

"I don't know."

Janet turned back to Allen. "So we've got to watch the semi until Garcia's on board?"

"Yeah. She'll want its exact location. We've got to do everything we can to accommodate her. After she agrees to help, she can have some police agency stop the semi and search it. Then we help Angelita get to where she wants to go." He turned to Angelita. "Does that work for you?"

She nodded.

"Do you have family in the US? Do you have a phone number to call?"

"Yes, I do."

"Get some rest. We're probably going to be here a while."

An hour later the Jeep came back and dropped off the truck driver. He climbed up into the cab.

"I hope that was worth it," Janet said. "His bosses are going to be pissed."

Allen chuckled. "Serves him right, getting involved with slavers."

At 6:00 a.m., the semitruck drove away, headed north. Janet and Allen followed, Janet behind the wheel. At 8:00 a.m., Allen called Garcia's office landline telephone.

"Hello?"

"Good morning, Garcia. Do you know who this is?"

"How did you get this number?"

"Never lost it."

"If you're calling from a county lockup, you've wasted your call."

"I'm calling to put you on to an opportunity."

"Sounds like one of your cons."

"How would you like a major score against the Orange Hill Cartel?"

"Organized crime? If you're on the level, you need to call the FBI. We only do national security cases."

"Does gun running into Mexico and human trafficking into the US rise up to the level of national security?"

"I'm listening."

"We just liberated a group of undocumented women from the back of a semitruck. I'm going to put one of them on the phone." He handed the phone to Angelita.

Angelita and Garcia spoke in Spanish. Then Angelita handed the phone back to Allen.

"Okay," Garcia said, "you've got my attention."

"We're following a Manning Brothers Freight semitruck north on Interstate 25 from El Paso heading toward Albuquerque. The driver doesn't know that his secret cargo has escaped. If you stop him, you'll find a hidden compartment in the front end of his trailer. The women are gone, but the mattresses and other evidence of occupation are all there. That should give you probably cause to search all the Manning Brothers trucks going south to Mexico or north from the border."

"What's the license plate number?"

Allen read it off.

"If you're jerking my chain, you will live long enough to regret it."

An hour later, a New Mexico state police cruiser pulled over the Manning Brothers truck. Allen, Janet, and Angelita drove by.

"Will it work?" Janet asked.

"I don't know," Allen replied. He turned to Angelita. "Thanks for your help." He handed her $200. "How about if we drop you off in Albuquerque?"

"At the bus station?"

"Sure."

"Give her a phone," Janet said, "so she'll have a real chance."

Allen got a burner phone out of the glove box and turned toward Angelita. "This phone is clean. Never been used. It's good until the end of the month. Don't call anyone until after we drop you off." He handed it to her.

"*Gracias.*"

BACK IN ROCKY SHORE, Missouri, Singh was in his office at the bank, putting on his suit coat, when he got a call from the bank examiner, Carl Thompson, on his burner phone. "Yes," he said.

"I've been moved off your bank."

"Why?"

"Don't know. It happens. I've been assigned to a complicated audit in St. Louis, so it looks legit."

"Who's getting our bank?"

"My assistant."

"Missy Drake? But she's a straight arrow."

"Your books look completely correct. The usual number of small discrepancies. Nothing more."

"You sure we can't be caught?"

"My reputation is on the line with yours. Everything is fine."

"So you're out, then?"

"No, I'm still in for a piece of the pie."

"How do you figure that?"

"Knowledge is power. And next month I'll be expecting you to get caught up with what you owe me." Thompson ended the call.

Singh put away his burner and called Olivia on his office line. "Hello?"

"Come to my office."

As soon as Olivia shut the door behind her, Singh filled her in. "Is Carl right? Are we in the clear?"

"I think we are," Olivia said. "But we ought to go through the trust accounts over the last year just to be sure. If she doesn't notice anything over the last year, she's not going to dig back further."

"That makes sense. How long have we got?"

"Ten days before their next visit."

"Is that enough time?"

"Not line by line, but I'll be able to check everything that matters."

"Get it done."

AFTER ALLEN and Janet dropped Angelita off at the downtown Albuquerque transit center, they drove west on Interstate 40 through the Laguna Pueblo Indian reservation until they spotted a roadside motel with a gas station at a dusty intersection within sight of the interstate. The place had stucco walls that looked like a touristy version of a 1950s hacienda.

"Two cars parked in front of rooms," Janet said.

"The gas pumps look like they work."

"Hooray!"

"Oh, ye of little faith."

"Wonder if there's internet?"

Allen glanced at his phone. "We have phone service."

Janet went into the convenience store/office. An older man wearing a cowboy hat stood behind the counter.

"You know there's no tourist stuff right here? Access is two more exits down."

"We like to stay away from crowds."

"You came to the right place."

"Where's the nearest restaurant?"

"There's a place usually open for breakfast and lunch about two miles south."

"But no dinner?"

He shook his head.

"Where's the nearest dinner place?"

"Two exits west."

Janet booked a room for two nights and paid with cash. They parked in front of their room and rolled their bags in. The drapes and the bedspread were sun faded, but the room was clean. Allen turned on the TV to a local channel.

Janet set her roller bag on the bed and unzipped it. "How long do you think it will take before we know something?"

"Within a couple of days, I would think. The Feds will have to move fast if they want to disrupt the cartel. As soon as the cartel discovers their truck has been seized, they'll stop moving merchandise until they think they're in the clear. So either the Feds are going to get the job done, or we'll have to try something else.

At 5:30 p.m., they drove west two exits to civilization. A supper club, and all-day breakfast place, and a Subway sandwich shop sat on three corners of the intersection, the cars in the parking lots featuring mostly out-of-state license plates. On the last corner, a food truck advertised tacos with beans and rice. They pulled to the side of the food truck where they couldn't possibly be filmed by the cameras at the other restaurants and ordered the daily special—two beef tacos, pinto beans, and rice. They sat down at a picnic table under an umbrella.

Janet took a bite of her taco. "Not bad."

"Probably the best food at this intersection," Allen replied.

After they ate, they put their trash in the barrel and drove back down to their motel. Allen turned on the TV and sat on the bed with his back against the headboard. The local news was about to start. Janet sat down beside him. Some national news, some state news, some Indian Country news. No federal or state contraband busts. Allen turned off the TV.

"Too soon. They have to get a warrant and get organized to stop as many trucks as possible. Tomorrow at the earliest."

"Think Sean and Phyllis are following us?"

"No one's following us. We popped up on the surveillance cameras in Jackson, but we were only there a day and a half. We might have popped up at the bus station in Albuquerque, but that's halfway across the country from Wyoming. As long as we keep moving, and avoid cameras whenever we can, we're going to be hard to find."

The next day, watching the TV in their room, they saw a news story about three Manning Brothers trucks being stopped in New Mexico near El Paso, two going south and one going north. ATF agents stood in a warehouse next to folding tables loaded with rifles and pistols. FBI agents stood in front of a group of women whose faces had been blurred to protect their identities. "These seizures are part of an ongoing investigation of organized crime at the US-Mexico border. This was the work of a multi-agency task force, including the New Mexico State Police and ICE, putting in long hours over several months."

"Garcia came through," Allen said. "I've got to admit I had my doubts."

"Well, it's history now," Janet replied. "And the Orange Hill Cartel must be looking for someone to blame."

"They don't have to look," Allen replied. "Mr. Wishes was their guy on the ground, so they're going to blame him."

"He's got to be in a rage."

"Pretty soon he won't be thinking straight, and we'll walk him right into a jail cell. And the cartel is going to be so busy dealing with the fallout that they won't have time to think about us."

They packed their bags and took Interstate 40 headed toward Flagstaff, Arizona. "We need more info on this last job," Allen said. "I'm calling Billy."

He answered on the second ring.

"Hey, Traveling Man, I see you've been busy."

"So far so good. Hey, Billy, I need more info on the Arizona drug smuggling."

"Like I said, Orange Hill takes shipments of fentanyl in the Arizona desert."

"How and where?"

"A Mexican cartel controls that area."

"All the better. No civilians in the way."

"Even if you manage to get away clean, you won't make a penny. You try to sell the drugs; the cartel will be all over you."

"We don't need to make money. We need the drugs to set a trap."

"It's your call."

"What part of the Arizona desert?"

"There's an empty area between the Barry M. Goldwater Air Force Range and the Organ Pipe Cactus National Monument. Deadly ground if you get lost or break down."

"Have you got any connections down there?"

"I know a few coyotes."

"Hook us up."

"Maybe I should keep looking."

"Any job you find involving Mr. Wishes is going to be crazy dangerous. I like our odds on this one."

"Okay. Let me know when you get to Phoenix." He ended the call.

"That was the easy part," Janet said. "Billy makes money with us."

"And he likes us," Allen added.

"But now you have to convince Garcia."

"She just got a win on the guns and human trafficking. Drug interdiction sells itself."

"We'll see."

THE MANNING BROTHERS Freight Company driver walked out of the federal courthouse in Albuquerque, New Mexico, accompanied by his lawyer. "Don't say anything about the incident to anyone. You didn't know about the compartment. All you do is drive where management tells you to drive."

"Yes, sir."

"There's your ride." The lawyer led him to a black Suburban parked in a metered parking place along the street.

A man in a gray suit got out of the front seat and opened the back door.

"Where we going?" the truck driver asked.

"We're going to debrief you and take you to a hotel."

"Remember," the lawyer said, "you can't leave the county."

"Gotcha," the driver said. He climbed into the back seat. A sallow-faced man in a black suit was sitting on the left side, and a man wearing business casual sat in the third row. Gray suit closed the door and got into the front.

The truckdriver turned to the man on his left. "Who are you?"

"Mr. Wishes."

"You guys from the front office?" the truck driver asked.

"You might say that. Where did you go when you left your truck unattended at AJ's Travel Center?"

"I didn't go anywhere."

"You know there're cameras all over that place, right? I can show you footage of you leaving."

"Went to a motel."

"With who?"

"My girlfriend. I'd been on the road two weeks. She came down to see me."

"Does she know anything about your extra cargo?"

"Are you crazy? No. Absolutely not."

"Well, we're all in hot water now."

"I know. I can't believe it happened. I'm as sorry as I could be about it. Thanks for getting me a lawyer."

"Thanks for being so candid."

Mr. Wishes nodded. The man in the third row slipped a garroting wire over the truckdriver's head and pulled it tight around his neck using both hands. The truckdriver struggled, gasping and kicking. He tried to claw under the wire with his fingers. Blood trickled down into his shirt. His face turned blue. He stopped struggling.

"Pull over," Mr. Wishes said.

The Suburban pulled to the curb in front of an apartment building. Mr. Wishes got out. "I want him under eight inches of concrete."

"Yes, sir," Gray suit replied. "We got a spot picked out at a new freeway rest stop."

The Suburban drove away. A few minutes later, a yellow cab pulled up. "You're late," Mr. Wishes said.

"Traffic," the cab driver replied.

ANGELITA SAT on a worn-out sofa in the back room of a taxi stand in downtown Albuquerque. Her blouse was torn and she had a black eye. A Latino and an Anglo, both dressed in jeans and flannel shirts with the sleeves rolled up, slouched in the space between her and the door.

Mr. Wishes walked into the room. He looked at the men and then at Angelita.

"She's the one, boss," the Latino said.

Mr. Wishes wheeled an office chair over and sat down in front of her. "Looks like you've been smacked around." He tried to smile. "I'm sorry for that."

Angelita kept her eyes on the floor.

"I'm told you have an interesting story about how you got out of the truck. I want you to tell it to me. Look at me."

She looked up.

"No one will hurt you if you tell the truth."

"Okay. A man opened the door to the hidden compartment in the truck. He asked if we wanted to leave. He let everyone go."

"Where was the driver?"

"I don't know. He came back later."

"So then what happened?"

"The man took me to a truck. A woman was there."

"What kind of truck?"

She shook her head. "The kind with a back seat. It was silver. That's all I know."

"Continue."

"We sat there. The truck driver came back. We followed his truck. When it was day, the man called someone. I spoke to her in Spanish. She asked if I had crossed the border illegally. A little later, the police stopped the truck and we drove on to Albuquerque."

"And they gave you money and a phone?"

"*Si.*"

"What did the man look like?"

"Just average. Average build, normal haircut, no tattoos."

"And the woman?"

"*Muy hermosa*, even without makeup."

"Thank you." He rolled his chair back away from her. "Are you a troublemaker?"

"No, senior."

"Are you going to do what you're told until you pay off your debt for bringing you here?"

"Yes, sir."

"Good girl."

Mr. Wishes left the room, walked through the front office of the taxi stand and out into the blazing sun. The silver F-150 had been on the truck stop surveillance footage, but there was no clear view of the occupants. Now he knew for a fact it was the grifters. They hit his card game. Now they put the Feds on Orange Hill's gun smuggling and sex trafficking operation. He got into the first taxi. "Airport."

They stole over $100,000 out of his pocket, but they didn't make a dime disrupting the gun smuggling and sex trafficking. Why do it? They'd just cost Orange Hill between half a million and a million. The cartel might even have to move ports of entry and bribe a whole new set of border guards. Why were they doing this? What did they hope to achieve? This would only make more people want them dead. He texted Sean. *Grifters were in El Paso and Albuquerque.*

Sean replied: *We're on it.*

Before, the grifters were just a pain in the ass that needed to be eliminated, but now it was personal. The cartel was going to start questioning his competence. He wouldn't be able to take his full cut if they were watching too closely. And if the cartel found out how long the grifters have been evading him, they might begin to think he was too soft for any important jobs.

The taxi stopped at a traffic light. He wanted the grifters chained up in an old barn, two hard guys working on them with pliers and blow torches until they gave up all their secrets and whatever money they had squirreled away. That wouldn't make them even, but it would be a start.

10

The Travelers, Allen and Janet, took Interstate 17 south to Phoenix. It was after dark when they merged onto the AZ-303 and exited in Surprise, Arizona, west of the city. "We need the lowest, most disreputable motel we can find," Allen said.

Janet googled truck stops. "Got a likely suspect," she said. "Take the next right."

At an intersection beyond a Love's Travel Center, they pulled into the parking lot of the Lonesome Trail Truckstop and Motel. The motel was a long, one-story concrete block building with the office at the end near a large array of covered gas and diesel pumps. Six semi-trucks were parked under pole lights on the far side of the gas pumps, and young women in tiny shorts and T-shirts were moving between the trucks.

"Good find," Allen said. "Obvious prostitution and no cameras." He parked in front of the motel office.

"Do you think they'll tell you about the hourly rate?"

He chuckled. "I think you better come in with me."

A middle-age man with the predatory look of a pimp got up from his easy chair behind the counter when they came through the door.

"You folks lost?"

"No, we need a room," Allen said.

He looked Janet up and down. "How many days?"

"A week," Allen replied.

He nodded.

"Put us in a quiet room," Janet added.

"I can't guarantee anything, but the far end is usually the quietest."

They paid in cash for the week, took the key, drove down to the room, and rolled their bags in. The room smelled of cheap cleaner and marijuana. The sheets were thin and the towels were threadbare.

"I've been in better jail cells," Janet said.

"But you didn't have a key to the door," Allen replied. "Where can we get something to eat?"

Janet used her smartphone to search for restaurants. "There's a sports bar that's still open just north of here."

"Let's do it."

The parking lot was half-full at Little Red's Sports Bar and Bistro. Country music wafted in from speakers in the ceiling, and big-screen TVs hung from the walls. The hostess, a redhead wearing tight jeans, a white shirt, and a fringed red vest, led them to a booth. The menus were typical for such an establishment—burgers, chicken, barbeque, or steak. They ordered martinis.

"Are we going to do this job the way we pulled that job in upstate New York?" Janet asked.

"You mean the hijacking?"

"Yes."

"The first part, yes. We'll have to find the routes that the Mexicans use to come across the border, and then stake them out until we spot the Orange Hill Cartel's people. Then after we hijack the load, we'll use it as bait for the Feds."

"What if Garcia isn't interested?"

"Then we'll just have to keep running, putting together small jobs as we move along, until we're sure the Orange Hill Cartel has given up. But she's going to be interested. This could be a bigger deal than the gun smuggling."

They stopped talking while the server set down their food, steak salad for her and a pulled pork plate for him. After their server left, they continued.

"When will we talk to Garcia?"

"Tomorrow. No reason to wait. We'll use the same phone to make sure she picks up."

After they ate, they drove back to the Lonesome Trail Truckstop. A few minutes later, there was a knock at the door. Allen answered it. Janet stood behind the door with her Glock in her hand.

"Yeah?"

A thirtyish woman wearing cut-off jeans and a T-shirt with no bra stood with a six-pack of beer in her hand. "Do you need some cold beer?"

Allen shook his head no.

She shifted her hips. "Or something else to settle your nerves after a long day of driving?"

Janet stepped around the door, keeping her pistol behind her.

"Oh," the woman said. "Looks like I'm too late."

"Another time, Sugar," Janet said.

Allen shut the door. "Glad we got that out of the way. Hate for someone to bang on the door after we've gone to bed."

"The action in the parking lot could be going on most of the night. We should probably bring our gear inside just in case someone breaks into the truck."

THE NEXT MORNING, before they loaded their bags back into the truck, Allen called Garcia and put the phone on speaker.

"Hello?"

"Good morning, Garcia. How did you like that last tip?"

"I'd like to know what was in it for you."

"Just being a good citizen."

"I assume there's a reason for this call?"

"How would you like to bust a fentanyl smuggling gang?"

"I'm listening."

"The Orange Hill Cartel is receiving a load across the Arizona border in the Sonoran Desert sometime in the next month."

"How do you know that?"

"Came across the info."

"I came across some intel that Orange Hill is after you for ripping off their diamonds."

"Yeah, but that doesn't mean my info isn't true."

"I can't tie up resources and mount an operation on your say-so. On the gun smuggling and human trafficking, you had a witness."

"But you would be interested if I could get some proof?"

"I'd be happy to bust the Orange Hill Cartel."

"I'll be in touch." He ended the call and turned to Janet. "What do you think?"

"I think we're on our own. But we always are, so we might as well see if this will work."

They called Billy.

"I contacted a few guys," he said. "Your best bet is a coyote named Ernesto Ramirez. His crew only moves migrants, so he doesn't care about the drug angle. He'll meet you tomorrow or the next day in Ajo, Arizona, which is north of the Organ Pipe Cactus National Monument."

Janet pulled up a map on her phone. "There's nothing down there."

"Just stuff that will kill you."

"What have you told him about us?"

"That you aren't competitors, and I vouch for you. He'll be driving a Jeep Wrangler and will be parked outside an abandoned coffee shop between seven a.m. and nine a.m. in the south part of Ajo they call Mexican Town."

"Thanks, Billy," Allen said.

"Good luck."

MEANWHILE, at the National Defense Agency in Suitland, Maryland, just outside of Washington, DC, Garcia was on the phone with Tina

Han, the manager of the NDA's tech department. "Could you get a trace on that last call?"

"Too short, boss," Han replied. "All we know is that it bounced off a cell tower in Phoenix."

Garcia touched the small gold cross hanging from her neck. "Have we got surveillance capability in the area between Phoenix and the Mexican border?"

"How bad do you want it? I could reroute a satellite."

"Too expensive. This might just be a wild goose chase. Do you remember those thieves who call themselves the Travelers?"

"They were around the edges of the case involving the diamond smuggling and the white nationalists, weren't they?"

"Exactly. If they're down in southern Arizona, do we have an economical way to track them remotely?"

"We've got a computer program that can scrape the public surveillance cameras. It's not perfect, but we won't be breaking the law."

"How much time is involved?"

"We could have it up and running this morning. We can use the video we have of them from the diamond smuggling case to set the images we're looking for. It will probably take a few days to start tracking them, depending on how many cameras they go by."

"Then you better get started."

ALLEN AND JANET left the Lonesome Trail Truckstop and took AZ-85 south through the Barry M. Goldwater Air Force Range to Ajo in the Sonoran Desert. "Beautiful little resort town," Janet said.

"Too many surveillance cameras," Allen replied.

They pulled into the parking lot of the Sonoran Desert Inn. Janet put on a long blonde wig and dark sunglasses. Allen put on a brimmed sunhat and sunglasses. "The last time we could have been on a camera was in Albuquerque, so the chances of being tracked are miniscule," he said.

"But we're going to have to use a credit card here."

"Still worth the risk. Especially when we can disappear back to the Lonesome Trail Truckstop. What's our cover story?"

"We're here visiting the Organ Pipe Cactus National Monument to celebrate our wedding anniversary," Janet said.

"That's us. Nature-loving environmentalists."

They checked into the hotel and used their Bixby credit card to secure their suite. Then they drove south through Mexican Town and ended up at the Mine Outlook Visitors Center, where they got out of the truck to look at the old pit mine.

"Someone made a lot of money here back in the day," Janet said.

"It's big hole all right. Continue to the Ajo Museum?"

"Let's save it."

As they drove back up Indian Village Road, Janet noticed an adobe shack with a Café sign attached to the gable. "That must be the coffee shop," she said. "Doesn't look like it's been open for a long time."

"Isolated. Perfect place for an ambush. If Billy wasn't vouching for Ramirez, I wouldn't meet there."

THE CONTRACT KILLERS, Sean and Phyllis, were sitting on a sofa in a hotel suite in Albuquerque, New Mexico, watching the news on the TV when Terry called.

Sean answered the phone and put it on speaker. "Terry, what have you got?"

"Spotted your targets in Ajo, Arizona."

"When?"

"Just now."

"Where is that?"

"In the south, near the Mexican border."

"Keep on them."

"How about 'good job, Terry? Knew you'd do it.'"

"How about 'your check is in the mail'?"

"I'll be in touch."

Phyllis got out her phone and clicked on her map app. "Ajo,

Arizona, is south of Phoenix and west of Tucson so far in the middle of nowhere that the air force has a bomb testing range nearby."

"They're definitely setting up another scam. Let's get packed and get moving."

THE NEXT MORNING, at 7:30 a.m., Allen and Janet pulled up to the abandoned coffee shop in Mexican Town. Weeds were growing up through cracks in the parking lot, and the building was dark inside. "Now we wait," Allen said. He and Janet wore Kevlar vests under their jackets. Their Glock pistols lay in their laps.

"I'll circle the building," Janet said.

She climbed out of the truck and walked slowly off toward the right side of the shack, pistol down at her side. The side window was boarded up and a few dry weeds grew in the gravel. Around the back, the door, which was chained and padlocked, stood open a few inches, like someone had tried to kick it in. On the left side of the building, a zigzag crack ran from the foundation to the roof.

As she started back across the gravel parking lot, she saw a Jeep Wrangler coming down the road toward them. Allen climbed out of the truck and tucked his pistol in the back of his pants. "We're up," he said.

The rusted white Jeep pulled to a stop beside their truck. A fat man wearing cowboy boots and a Stetson stepped out. "You Allen?"

Allen nodded. "You Ernesto Ramirez?"

They shook hands.

"This is my wife, Janet."

"Ma'am." Ramirez tipped his hat. "Billy said you needed some information."

"That's right," Allen replied.

"I'm listening."

"We want to know which trails the drug smugglers use to bring their cargo across the border down here."

"Why?"

"We're not going to interfere, if that's what you're concerned about. We're interested in a customer of theirs that they're going to meet on this side."

"Information isn't free."

"Didn't expect it to be. I've got four thousand dollars for the answers we need."

"Let me get a map." He dug around in his glove box, found a topographical map of the area, and opened it on the hood of the Jeep.

"Okay. We're here." He pointed to Ajo. "Straight south is Organ Pipe National Monument, which is loaded up with tourists. To the north is the air force bombing practice range, also a bad idea. And if you take Bates Well Road south to El Camino Del Diablo, you'll end up at Camp Grip, a border patrol outpost almost at the border. To the west of it, there's a pass through the hills that goes north on the other side of this ridge. Migrants can't come up this way. Too difficult. But four-wheelers can make it through this notch," he pointed at a place between two ridges, "and then cross the air force range in the night without drawing attention."

"They're not worried about unexploded ordnance?"

"They've got a safe path." He continued. "Then they pop up at this rest stop just west of the town of Sentinel on Interstate 8."

"They have to come up through here?" Allen pointed at a spot on the map north of the Air Force range.

"No other way. Too many border patrol agents on the other side of the ridges to the east."

"How active are the drug smugglers?"

"It's an ongoing business."

"And they always go to this rest stop?"

"The local cops are on the payroll."

Allen reached into his jacket pocket and pulled out a wad of one-hundred-dollar bills. "We've never met."

"You're crazy to set up anywhere near the cartel's route."

"You're probably right."

"*Adios.*"

Allen and Janet waited for the Jeep to disappear before the got into their truck and drove back into Ajo. "Think he'll sell us out to the drug cartel?" Janet asked.

"I don't know. I just think setting up at the rest stop is worth the risk. We're going to have to be on the alert anyway."

"Here's where the job adds moving parts."

He nodded. "We'll need a rotation of rental cars and some light disguises. Where's the nearest touristy town to the rest stop on Interstate 8?"

Janet looked at her map app. "Gila Bend."

"Let's use that as our base."

"There're two independent motels."

"The best one without surveillance cameras."

"Looks like that would be the Gila River Inn. To be on the safe side, we'll have to go up toward Phoenix to rent a car."

"How far?"

"Forty-five minutes or so."

"That's within reason. And we've still got a few days left at the Lonesome Trail Truckstop if we need to change up in a hurry." Allen pulled up to a stoplight on Solana Avenue. "Once we have the fentanyl, where do we want to hide it?"

"How about an Airbnb in a residential neighborhood?"

"Not in Gila Bend."

"No." The traffic light turned green. "And if we're getting rental cars from Phoenix, we don't want to use a place up there."

"Or anyplace else we've already been. Between the rest stop and the car rental places, we're probably going to end up on some surveillance cameras."

"It's Russian roulette now."

"We always knew it was going to get tricky when we moved to set the trap. To hide the fentanyl, we need a spot we're only going to the one time. We make sure we don't get seen, and we don't go back."

Janet clicked on her map app. "How about Tucson? It's big enough to hide in and has lots of roads leaving town if we need to take off in a hurry."

"Find an Airbnb in a quiet neighborhood."

. . .

TWO HOURS LATER, the contract killers Sean and Phyllis were on Arizona highway 85 driving south through the Barry Goldwater Air Force Range.

"This landscape is desolate, but there're no bomb craters," Phyllis said.

"They must avoid the highway."

"I was hoping to see a few."

"Big ones?"

"Like moon craters." She looked at her phone. "We'll be there in about thirty minutes."

"Better call Terry," Sean said.

Terry picked up on the second ring. "What's up?"

"What have you got on our targets? We're getting close to Ajo, and we don't want to roll in blind," Sean said.

"There're a few surveillance cameras in town, but they haven't been on them. There're no cameras on the Ajo-Gila Bend Road, so I'm running a program on the cameras up at Gila Bend, just in case. I'm hoping they'll turn up at a gas station or convenience store. As soon as I know anything, I'll be in touch."

Sean ended the call. "Wish we had better intel."

"At least the grifters don't know this car," Phyllis replied.

11

That evening, after dark, Allen and Janet were sitting in a GMC Yukon with the seats reclined on the south side of the Interstate 8 rest stop west of Sentinel, Arizona. They were dressed in dark clothes and Kevlar, their AR-15 rifles pointed down in the floorboards beside them. The occasional car whooshed by on the freeway, a few pulling into the rest stop to use the facilities, and the time ticked by. Shortly after 2:00 a.m., a panel van pulled into the rest stop and backed into a parking space on the south side of the parking lot. Then they heard the noise of a small engine approaching from the south, and saw a four-wheeler, lights off, as it came into the light dome of the rest stop.

They watched through binoculars as the four-wheeler stopped at the back of the panel van. A Latino dressed in jeans and a work shirt got out of the van and opened its back doors. The two men on the four-wheeler loaded several boxes into the back of the van, shook hands with the van driver, and got back on the four-wheeler. The van driver got back in the van and drove off toward Gila Bend.

"That wasn't Orange Hill," Janet said. "Those guys all knew each other."

"Yeah," Allen said. "That was an inhouse transfer. But at least we know Ramirez wasn't shining us on. Let's go home."

SEAN'S SMARTPHONE BUZZED. He rolled over in bed and looked at the screen. 3:00 a.m. call from Terry. "Hope this is good news."

"I've found your targets."

"Where?"

"Caught them on the camera at the rest stop on Interstate 8 west of Sentinel, Arizona."

"What are they driving?"

"GMC Yukon."

"Which way did they go when they left?"

"Toward Gila Bend. Surveillance log indicates that they've been sitting at the rest stop since shortly after 8:00 p.m."

"Did they leave in a hurry?"

"No."

"So they're set up there?"

"Looks like it."

AT THE FREEDOM BANK AND TRUST in Rocky Shore, Missouri, bank examiner Missy Drake, a Black woman wearing a tan pantsuit, sat in Singh's office, facing him across the desk.

"Congratulations on your promotion," Singh said.

"Thank you," she replied.

"We've got the usual conference room for you to work in with the computer set up to access all the trust data. Any assistance you need, just ask Olivia."

"Great. Let me get started."

AT 3:45 P.M., Olivia Blevins knocked on the door to the conference room that Missy Drake was working in and went in. "Ms. Drake," she said, "how's your first day going?"

Missy sat back in her chair and cracked her neck. "Just fine."

"I'd like to take you out to dinner, if that's okay."

"I can't accept gratuities," she said.

"If you'd like some company, we can go out together and each pay our own way."

"I think I'll just go back to my hotel and order room service, call home and talk to my kids."

"If you change your mind anytime while you're here, just give me a holler."

Olivia left the conference room and went upstairs to Singh's office.

Singh looked up from his laptop computer. "Well?"

"We're not going to be able to win her over. She won't even accept a free meal."

"I told you." He closed his laptop. "You looked through the trust accounts? Everything is as it should be?"

"It all looks great on the surface. As long as she doesn't do a deep dive into an account we've been in, we should be all right."

"I don't like this."

"If we pass muster this time, all the old transactions will be in the clear. She won't be looking at them again. The problem is what to do going forward. Without her cooperation, we're not going to be able to skim the trusts using the methods we used before."

"There's got to be a way to slip it past her."

"What about having someone from Elemental Security investigate her? She looks squeaky clean, but that might be because she's covering up something in her past."

"Okay, if she doesn't find anything in her audit, I'll have Dido set something up."

AFTER OLIVIA LEFT Singh's office, he opened his laptop. Too many *ifs*. He clicked on his Tor Browser and input the internet address of the Bank of Geneva. Then he input the password to his numbered account. No one knew about this account. If Drake discovered their embezzlement, he wasn't going to jail. He could liquidate his mutual fund account, move it to the Geneva account, and disappear. But maybe he wouldn't have to. Maybe, worst case scenario, he could put the blame on Olivia. Claim that the most he was guilty of was trusting her.

He closed his numbered account and exited his Tor Browser. He was just being paranoid. Olivia was right. There was probably nothing to worry about. He was a long way from having to leave the country. Lots of choices before it came down to that.

But more importantly, in the short term, would they be able to find a way to get Drake to cooperate? Or were they done skimming the trust accounts? Where would he get the extra income he needed? Elemental Security was slowly building a client base. In three or four years, it might generate the extra money he needed. But he didn't have three or four years. He needed the money now, every month, just to stay out of debt. There had to be a way to get the money without touching his retirement fund.

OVER THE NEXT seven days the Travelers, Allen and Janet, lay in the dark at the rest stop in different rental cars and watched the four-wheeler make its transfer to various trucks and vans, but it always seemed to be an inhouse transfer.

On the eighth day, the night was shaping up to be another false alarm. Two semitrucks were parking in the truck parking and three passenger cars has stopped to use the restrooms. "I'm going to the ladies' room," Janet said.

"You're going to look very suspicious in Kevlar and boots."

"My back teeth are floating." She pulled off her Kevlar vest. "I'll keep a lookout for surveillance cameras."

She kept to the shadows as she made her way across the parking lot to the tourist center. The doors to the restroom section were open. She went into the women's restroom. It was dirty from a full day's use: toilet paper and paper towels on the floor, dirty sinks, a stopped-up toilet, but she found a clean toilet seat to sit on. When she was done, she flushed and came out of the stall.

Phyllis, dressed in dark clothes and holding a Glock pistol, stood between her and the door. She glanced over her shoulder. Sean was behind her.

"No need to get shot in here," Phyllis said. "Just come along with us. Let the future take care of itself."

Janet ran straight at Phyllis, but Sean sprang after her, grabbed her hair from behind, and swung her into the cement block wall. She kicked and punched, but they dragged her down to the floor, Sean's hands around her throat.

When she woke, she was lying in the back seat floorboard of Sean and Phyllis's Highlander, tape over her mouth and her wrists and ankles zip-tied. Her head was pounding. She could hear road noise. She opened her eyes and looked around. It was still dark.

"There she is," Phyllis said. "I was beginning to think that Sean had choked you a little too long."

Sean chuckled.

"We're going to be hanging onto you until we get your man," Phyllis said. "Don't cause us any trouble, and we'll make it quick when the time comes."

Janet grunted.

"There's no getting away," Sean said. "Only dying clean or messy. You decide."

MEANWHILE, Allen was still sitting in the parking lot of the rest stop. He was antsy, his head swiveling at any movement in his peripheral vision. Where was she? Something must have gone very wrong. There was no way she was in the bathroom this long. He kept glancing at the tourist center, but no one was going in or out. He checked his pistol's magazine to make sure it was fully loaded and then started to open his truck door when his phone buzzed. He looked at the screen. Janet. "Hello?"

"We've got your girl," the voice said. "She's in excellent condition, only a few scuff marks from collecting her."

"What have you got in mind, Sean?"

"So you know my name. Wonderful. There's a historic landmark —Dateland Ranch House—west of Stanwix. You meet us there at 8:00 a.m. tomorrow."

"Why not today?"

"Because we like tomorrow better. Don't bother to try to set up on us, we'll already be there."

"If one hair on her head is out of place, I'll kill you both."

"That's what I like, big balls and attitude. It'll be a pleasure to kill you."

"Tomorrow, then."

Allen ended the phone call. Was Janet still alive? Yes. They needed her to give proof of life if he asked for it, otherwise he wouldn't walk into the ambush. Was there still only two of them? If they were both at the meet and Janet wasn't with them, he'd have to leave Phyllis alive until he could find out where Janet was being held.

He got out his phone and googled Dateland Ranch House. It was a graffitied stone ruins in the desert off Interstate 8. Excellent place for an ambush. No time to call Billy and find some help. He was on his own. He drove out of the rest stop and headed toward Gila Bend. They had Janet, and he had one chance to get her back. He needed to find a way to get the upper hand.

SEAN AND PHYLLIS drove up to Sullivan's Self Storage, four long cement block buildings surrounded by a chain link fence topped with razor wire. An abandoned Mobile gas station with boarded up windows sat across the road. There was nothing else for miles in any direction except for chaparral and stunted trees. Sean input his code on the keypad at the gate and the gate slid open. He parked their Highlander in front of a self-storage unit at the far end of the leftmost building. Phyllis got out and lifted the garage door. Sean jerked Janet out of the back seat and pulled her hopping along on her zip-tied feet into the ten-feet by ten-feet storage unit. A bare mattress lay in one corner, next to a gallon jug of water, an empty bucket, and a box of peanut butter cracker sandwiches.

"Your new home," Phyllis said. She turned on the overhead light.

Sean dragged her to the mattress and gave her a shove.

Janet rolled over on the mattress to look up at them and peeled the tape off her mouth. "How can I use the bucket with my ankles zip-tied?"

"You'll find a way," Sean replied.

"You won't be here long," Phyllis added.

"What if you two don't make it back?"

"You better hope we do," Sean said. "Kind of heat out here, you won't last two days."

They closed the garage door. Janet heard a padlock click shut. She waited for a few minutes to make sure they were gone. Would they come back? There was no way of telling. She looked around the room. The back wall and side walls were concrete block. There was an air duct in the ceiling, but it was too small and too high. Her only hope was the garage door. She inched her way over to the left side of the door, scooting on her butt. The door track had a blunt edge on it, but it was heavy-duty steel. She ran her ankle zip-tie back and forth against the edge, pushing hard with her bent legs until it popped. Then she did the same for the zip-tie on her wrists.

She rubbed the red marks on her wrists. Sean and Phyllis probably figured that she would get out of the zip-ties, but they probably didn't think she would do it so fast. Not that it mattered. The garage door was locked. She sat down on the mattress, drank some water and ate a few peanut butter crackers. There had to be some way of bypassing the garage door. She needed to think.

ALLEN LAY IN BED, tossing and turning. He'd been up all night and needed to get some rest for the work ahead, but he couldn't sleep with Janet kidnapped, so he got up, took a shower, and went for breakfast at a nearby coffee shop. He wondered if Janet was in the trunk of a car, or if they'd put her in a stash house—whether they'd beaten her or raped her. Well, he could only kill them once. He'd just have to be satisfied with that. It was almost 10:00 a.m. The day was going to be a scorcher. The coffee shop was empty except for three people working at their laptop computers. He bought a ready-made breakfast burrito and a large coffee and sat down at a table by the front window.

Tomorrow morning at Dateland Ranch House was going to be a straight-up shoot out. The Google pictures showed open terrain—a bad place for a gun fight, particularly if you were outnumbered. To face Sean and Phyllis alone, he'd need heavy body armor with arm and leg coverage. And some luck. But he didn't have any choice. Janet would be dead if he waited too long. After he finished his coffee, he googled gun stores in the Phoenix area and found one on the east side with a complete line of protective gear.

He drove away from the coffee shop and took Arizona 85 up to Interstate 10 into Phoenix. He didn't think he was being followed, but he took an exit, circled around through a shopping district, and got back on the I-10. If anyone was following him, he'd lost them now.

THE CONTRACT KILLERS, Sean and Phyllis, parked in the parking lot at the Dateland Ranch House. There were two pickup trucks and a car parked there, and about half a dozen people strolling through the graffiti-tagged ruins of several adobe buildings. Sean and Phyllis walked up past a tumbled-down stone wall and then turned around to look at the parking lot.

"One way in, one way out," Sean said.

"The parking lot is completely open. Easy rifle shot from here."

"And if he's hiding behind a vehicle, we can shoot out the tires. Keep him from getting away."

"I'm so glad we're almost done with this job," Phyllis said.

"Not taking chances."

"Kevlar and helmets?"

"Yes, indeed."

"What about the female?"

"After he's dead? We're not cruel. One shot to the head."

"That'll make it a closed casket."

"That's the line of work she chose."

ALLEN GOT out of his truck in the parking lot of Complete Firearms and Accessories. Hunting clothes and boots were on the left side of the store. Police tactical gear and body armor were on the right. A glass counter across the back contained handguns, and rifles hung from the wall behind.

A hard-bodied man with a crewcut stood behind the counter, his shirt tucked into his khaki pants and a Smith & Wesson holstered at his side. "Can I help you?"

Allen smiled. "How you doing?"

"Living the dream."

"I'll bet." Allen walked back to the counter. "I'm looking for heavy-duty body armor. Torso, arms, legs, helmet."

The man stepped out from behind the counter. "You came to the right place."

"Glad to hear it."

The man led him to a display of body armor on the right wall, where he pointed at a vest. "I'm sure you know the trade-offs. More stopping power means increased weight."

Allen nodded.

"And the arm and leg guards will impede your movement."

"I understand. I still want the most stopping power."

"Very well." He picked out a vest, arm and leg guards, and a helmet. "These are the best. They're not cheap, though."

Allen smiled. "I'm worth it."

"Let's try them on for size." The man helped Allen put on the body armor.

"You've got a good eye," Allen said. "This is a good fit."

"Are you law enforcement? There's a law enforcement discount."

"No such luck." Allen took off the body armor and handed the man his Tom Bixby credit card.

. . .

JANET STOOD on the right side of the garage door, the opposite side from the padlock, and pushed the roller side-to-side in the garage door track. If she could flex the track away from the roller, maybe she could pop the roller out of the track. If she did that to four rollers, she could probably squeeze through the gap and get out of here. She took off her shirt and wrapped her hands with it. Then she braced her legs into the floor and pushed against the track. No dice. She only moved it an eighth of an inch, maybe. She couldn't flex the track far enough.

She looked around the room. A pry bar, a claw hammer, even a long screwdriver would help. But the room was empty. Except for the latrine bucket. She inspected the handle, which was a heavy-duty, stiff wire with a plastic sleeve for a hand hold. She popped the ends of the handle out the plastic pivots in the bucket. How could she use it as a lever?

She put the ends of the wire handle into the far side of the garage door track and levered the handle against the near side of the track. She pushed on the handle as hard as she could. The ends popped out of the track, scratching her forearm. Blood trickled down onto her hand. Shit.

She lay down on her back and tried kicking the track off the roller, but all that did was make a lot of noise. She stood up and examined the bucket handle again. If she could bend it, get the ends closer together, maybe then it would be a more effective lever. She went to the mattress, pushed one side of the handle down into the foam to stabilize it, and bore down with all her weight. The handle bowed down a few inches, but when she let go, it sprang back into its original shape.

She went back to the garage door and tried to lever the roller out of the track again, watching very carefully to make sure the ends of the wire handle didn't pop out of the far side of the track. Nothing. She lay down and kicked at the track again, rattling the garage door. She had to get out of here.

A voice called out. "Hello?"

Janet answered. "I'm in here!"

"You're inside the storage unit?"

"Yes."

"There's a lock on the door. How did you end up inside?"

"Can you break the lock and open the door?"

"Hold on."

Janet pulled on her shirt. A few minutes passed. Then she heard a loud snap. The garage door went up. Janet dropped into a defensive stance, fists balled and ready to punch. A potbellied, bearded guy wearing leather and a biker vest stood in front of the door with a pair of bolt cutters in his hand. He looked into the unit—mattress, bucket, water bottle.

"Jesus Christ," he said. "Who put you in there?"

Janet relaxed. "Trust me, my friend, the less you know the better."

She stepped out of the unit. An old pickup truck sat in the aisle with its driver's door open. Power tools, bicycles, and a few large cardboard boxes were piled in the back. She half-smiled. It looked like the biker was robbing storage units. "Thanks for your help. I'm not interested in knowing anything about your business. Can I borrow your phone?"

"You calling the cops?"

"No. They're the last people I want to see. I'm calling a ride."

He handed her his cell phone. She input Allen's number. His phone rang six times.

"Hello," he said.

"Hey, baby," she replied. "Glad you answer for random numbers."

"Where are you? Are you safe?"

"Yes, I am." She turned to the biker. "What's the name of this place?"

"Sullivan's Self-Storage."

She spoke into the phone. "Did you hear that?"

"I'm on my way," Allen said. "It's going to take a while."

She hung up and handed the phone back to the biker. "Thanks."

He nodded. "You need anything else?"

"My guy is coming."

"Well, I don't know you, and I don't know your man. So I'm getting out of here."

The biker got into his truck and disappeared down a row of storage units. Janet lowered the garage door and put the cut padlock back on the hasp. Then she trotted down to the entrance. The chain-link gate opened automatically. She sat down by the side of the road under the shade of a spindly tree.

An hour and a half later, Allen pulled over by the tree and Janet climbed into their F-150.

"Glad to see you." He patted her thigh.

"Glad to see you," she replied. She leaned over and kissed him.

"They hurt you?"

She filled him in on what happened.

"I'm so glad you're as lucky as you are."

"Me, too."

"Thought I might lose you."

"But you didn't." They kissed again.

"Now we get even." He put the truck in drive. "It's the OK Corral in the morning. Think they'll come back to check on you before then?"

"You don't have to go now."

"Already bought the body armor. Besides, I'm not going to pass up a chance to be the hunter instead of the hunted."

"What time?"

"Eight a.m., out at the Dateland Ranch House, an old ruins west of Sentinel on I-8."

"How bad is the setup?"

"About as bad a natural ambush as I've ever seen."

"It sounds like a bad idea."

"Remember the crazy guy in the full body armor who shot up the movie theater in Colorado?"

She nodded.

"That's the kind of armor I just bought."

"Still risky."

"Of course it's risky. Otherwise, Sean and Phyllis wouldn't be trying to get me to go there. But now there're two of us, which gives us the element of surprise. Maybe we won't be able to kill them, but we ought to be able to slow them down."

SEAN AND PHYLLIS sat in a booth in a Tex-Mex restaurant called Shooters, margaritas in front of them.

"Is it my imagination, or are a lot of folks in here eyeing us over?"

Sean smiled. "It's not your imagination. I think a lot of these people have never eaten in a restaurant with Black folks before."

"First time for everything," she replied.

"Yes, indeed. I'm keeping a watch on our SUV."

"You think someone's going to vandalize it?"

"Old habits die hard."

The server brought their plates. "Anything else?"

"We're good," Sean replied.

"Enjoy."

Phyllis put a fork of refried beans into her mouth. "Should we check up on the female?"

Sean shook his head. "She's not going anywhere. She has to die. The less contact we have with her, the better."

"Okay." She sipped her margarita. "Get out to Dateland Ranch House by 6:00 a.m.?"

"That should be early enough. Then we'll find out how much of our bill Orange Hill is willing to pay," Sean said.

"You mean Mr. Wishes, don't you?"

"I don't really trust him. I thought doing this job might open some more lucrative jobs, but, more and more, I'm thinking as soon as we've finished this job we want to stay clear of the Orange Hill Cartel."

"Fine by me. Do you still think we might end up with some of the grifters' money?"

"Maybe, but we don't know where they're staying, so at this point I'm not counting on it."

.   .   .

LATER, at the Gila River Inn, Allen and Janet lay intertwined in the dark on the king-size bed, the TV pattering on in the background.

"That was a close call," Allen said.

"Pure luck that I escaped," Janet replied. "I was in the worst position possible. If they murdered you, their next stop was going to be me. And if you murdered them, then I would die from heat and dehydration in the storage unit."

"Unless you yelled," Allen said.

"They chose a storage place in the middle of nowhere. Shouldn't have been anyone there."

"Except a thief."

"And he could just have ignored me."

"So many ways to lose." He kissed her. "But we only need one way to win."

"So we fuck them up tomorrow?"

"I'm so tired of having them on our backs. We don't even have to kill them. They're professionals. They've got no skin in the game except money. I'd settle for scaring them off."

"Think that will work?"

"Probably not, but I'll take a win no matter how we get it."

12

At 6:00 a.m., Allen and Janet drove out to a used car dealership in suburban Phoenix. Allen put on gloves and a facemask and climbed the fence at the back of the lot away from the surveillance cameras. An old, chrome bumper Dodge Dakota sat against the back of a maintenance building. He hotwired it. It started, the engine sounded okay, and it had half a tank of gas. He drove out of the lot, Janet following in the F-150. They went down interstate 8, exited at Sentinel, pulled into the parking lot of a public park, moved their gear over to the Dakota, and left the F-150.

"You sure this Dakota will get the job done?" Janet asked.

"This is Detroit iron, honey. It'll stop all the long range rounds, and if they're close enough to blast through it, that will be the least of our worries."

When they reached the Dateland Ranch House parking lot, Janet slid down in the seat. There was one car in the lot, the silver Highlander. They pulled up beside it. Allen got out of the cab of the Dakota, climbed into the back, and put on his body armor while lying in the truck bed. After he adjusted the chin strap on his helmet, he climbed out of the bed and strapped on his weapons. He carried an AR-15 rifle in his hands, a Glock was holstered on his hip, and a Mossberg pump-action shot gun hung at his side from a shoulder strap.

He started across the parking lot and up the path to the main ruins. A rifle slug thumped into his chest plate. Another glanced off his leg guard. He paused, and then slow-trotted for cover behind a pile of broken adobe. He was struck twice more before he reached the pile. He noted that the shots were coming from a gap between two sections of adobe wall and rapid-fired several rounds into the gap.

In the meantime, Janet lowered the passenger door window of the truck, pushed the door open, and rested a sniper rifle on the window ledge. When Allen stopped firing, she looked through her rife scope, casting over the main ruins for a shot. She spotted a bit of pants leg through a hole in the adobe wall and fired. She was a couple of inches off to the right. The pants leg disappeared.

Allen ran for a three-foot-high section of tumbled-down wall. A shot glanced off his helmet, causing him to lurch right. Another shot caught him in the lower part of his front plate. He slid to the ground behind the tumbled-down wall, dust rising around him.

Janet spotted two gaps in the high wall in the distance and fired into both of them. Return fire smashed into the truck door.

Allen jumped up and ran for the right side of the main wall, lurching along like Frankenstein's monster, hoping to outflank Sean and Phyllis and create a shot for Janet. Once he cleared the corner, he crept along the broken wall, keeping his head down, until he reached a gap. He could hear Janet firing her rifle. He wheeled left through the gap, spraying fire from the AR-15.

Sean and Phyllis, both wearing Kevlar, dove to the ground and focused all their fire on Allen. Allen backed around the side wall, pulled his spent magazine and inserted a fresh one. When he came around the corner again, they were gone. He whistled, one long, one short. Janet stopped firing. He moved at a crouch toward the spot where Sean and Phyllis had been lying. When he got there, he saw a small puddle of blood and drips of blood leading away from the wall and farther into the ruins. He trailed the blood through a doorway, where it stopped. He scanned the surrounding ruins. Nothing. He hunkered down with his back against the wall and waited, his rife at the ready. If they were hidden nearby, and they moved, he might get a shot.

After ten long minutes, he got up and walked back out through the rubble. Janet was in the driver's seat by the time be got back to the truck.

She called out to him. "Any joy?"

"One of them is bleeding. It just got to the point where trying to wait them out seemed like a waste of time."

She started the truck. "Get in."

"Hold on a second." Allen pulled his Glock and shot through two of the Highlander's tires.

Janet chuckled.

Allen climbed into the passenger's side. "They're having a bad day."

They drove back to Sentinel to the public park. It was empty. They took off their tactical gear, moved their gear back into the F-150, and wiped down the Dodge Dakota. Within twenty minutes they were back on the freeway headed toward Gila Bend, Allen behind the wheel.

"Sean and Phyllis know we're set up at the Sentinel rest stop," Janet said.

"Yeah, it's the weak link, but there's not much we can do, except watch our backs and hope the Orange Hill fentanyl comes across the border sooner rather than later."

"Do we even know if our current information is correct?"

"Call Billy."

Allen handed Janet his phone. She input the number and put the phone on speaker.

"What's up?" Billy said.

"We're not finding the Orange Hill Cartel," Janet said.

"The info is the same," he said. "Big shipment of fentanyl coming from a Mexican cartel. It hasn't happened yet."

"When is it supposed to happen?"

"Soon. That's all I know."

"Okay, Billy. If you hear anything more precise, let us know."

She ended the call. "Maybe we're not at the right place."

"Why would the drug crew risk moving to another location to get rid of their product? They control the rest stop and the desert. They want to off-load at the least risky place for them. Their own product —they have to drive it away. But they don't have to risk the state police or border patrol for someone else's load."

"If they're doing what makes sense."

"Let's give it another week."

AFTER ALLEN and Janet drove away from the Dateland Ranch House, Sean staggered out of the ruins, Phyllis over his shoulder in a fireman's carry, his left arm wrapped around her leg and his right hand clutching his rifle. He slid her into the passenger's seat of the Highlander, got the first aid kit out of the back seat, and bandaged her thigh.

"Not too bad," he said. "We'll get it cleaned up back at the motel."

"Sorry about that."

"Nothing to be sorry about. That was pure dumb luck. Could have been me."

"But it wasn't."

"We can take it easy a few days. Terry can keep a close watch on them. Either they're going to run or continue with their scam. If they continue, they're going to be watching for us at the rest stop, so we need to find another place we can set up on them, a place where they won't expect us."

Phyllis set her seat back. "We need a tow truck."

"Let's bag up our Kevlar and helmets first. We've got to make the flats look like vandalism."

"Beginning to think we're jinxed when it comes to these grifters."

"We're not jinxed," Sean said. "You wait and see. We're going to have our way with them before everything's said and done. If they continue with their scam, we're going to get some new opportunities."

"How did she escape from the storage unit? I've never seen anything like that."

"First time for everything."

"Should have killed her. We could have taken him alone. Especially if he wasn't thinking straight."

"We won't make the same mistake again," Sean said.

"No, we won't. Are we going to tell Mr. Wishes?"

"Absolutely not."

ON FRIDAY, Missy Drake met with Singh and Olivia in Singh's office. "I just wanted to give you the head's up," Missy said. "Some of Carl's notations on the trust accounts are confusing."

"Is there some kind of problem?" Singh asked.

"Probably not. Next month I'll dig into a couple of the accounts, just to be sure."

"But you were Carl's assistant," Olivia said. "You've been through these accounts many times."

"Carl was the primary," Missy replied. "I took his word. But now, it falls on me, so I need to be absolutely sure."

Singh nodded. "How big of a deal is it from your point of view?"

"It's probably nothing. I wouldn't worry about it."

They all shook hands. "See you next month," Singh said.

After Missy left the room, Singh turned to Olivia. "Call Dido. Put a team on Missy. We need to know everything there is to know about her. How many kids? How many fathers? Kids in trouble? Any aunts, uncles, siblings in jail or on probation? We've got to find something we can use against her before she comes back next month."

"I'll take care of it."

OVER THE NEXT SEVERAL DAYS, Dido systematically dug into Missy Drake's life. She was twice divorced. She had two kids, a twelve-year-old boy and an eight-year-old girl. They appeared to be normal kids. One ex worked construction, the other was a plumber. Both had remarried. Uncles and aunts were retired, owned their homes, no bill troubles. Dido called Rachel Simpson. "Take Kevin. I'm emailing you a background report on Missy Drake. Follow her around. See if there's anything to add to the report."

Five days later, Rachel called in.

"What have you got?"

"Drake drives her mom into Illinois to visit a weed store."

"A weed store? So what?"

"Legal in Illinois. Illegal in Missouri."

"Got proof?"

"Video."

"Anything else?"

"No."

"Come home and bring me the video."

Dido called Olivia and filled her in. "How do you want to proceed?"

"Send all the information and the video to me," Olivia said.

Later that afternoon, Olivia read Dido's report and watched the video. Missy and an older woman got out of a car in the handicapped parking in front of Herbal Sunshine Dispensary. They went inside. A few minutes later, they came out, the older lady carrying a store bag with the dispensary's name on it. Then they drove back into Missouri.

Olivia emailed Missy. The message said: *We need to talk.* She attached a copy of the video. An hour later, she received a response. *Where?*

Tomorrow at noon at the north parking lot to the Mississippi River Park.

When Olivia arrived at the park, Missy was already there. Olivia got out of her car, walked over to Missy's car and tapped on the driver's side window. Missy lowered it. "Get in," she said.

Olivia shook her head. "Let's sit over there on the bench." She indicated a wooden bench under a sprawling maple tree.

Missy got out of her car. They walked over to the bench without saying anything. "It's not what you think," she said.

"It's exactly what I think," Olivia replied. "You were aiding and abetting your mom in breaking Missouri's drug laws."

"My mom has chronic pain."

"I feel sorry for her and you, but that doesn't give you the right to break the law. Personally, I don't care if you buy weed products for your mom. But, then again, I don't work for the St. Louis Federal Reserve in a position of trust. They might take a dim view of breaking the federal drug laws."

"What do you want?"

"You want me to look the other way, and I want you to look the other way. It's that simple."

"I know what I want you to ignore. What do you want me to ignore?"

"Straight to the point. I like that. There are some details in the trust accounts that might not stand up to scrutiny. That's what I want you to ignore."

"It can't be anything obvious."

"Did you notice anything obvious when you examined the trust accounts?"

"No."

"Then no digging. You wash my hands, and I'll wash yours." She stood up. "Glad we had a chance to talk before everything turned to mud."

Missy watched Olivia drive away. Olivia, and probably Singh, were embezzling from the trust accounts. That had to be what was going on. So it was a quid pro quo. They'd keep quiet about the marijuana edibles if she kept quiet about their skimming. Which meant she had to become part of their conspiracy if she was going to protect her mom. How many more crimes would that entail and how long would she have to participate?

She walked back to the parking lot and got in her car. She hadn't committed any real crimes yet. She might lose her job over helping her mom, but she wouldn't go to prison for buying edibles in Illinois and transporting them back to Missouri. But if she looked the other way on a possible embezzlement, she was eventually going to get caught. Everyone did. Then what would her kids think of her? And who would take care of them if she went to prison? Not her mom. Not her exes.

She got out her phone and speed-dialed her boss before she could change her mind.

13

Three nights later, the Travelers, Allen and Janet, sitting in a Nissan Frontier at the Sentinel rest stop, watched the four-wheeler pull up beside a white Ford Transit Cargo Van. A white guy wearing painter's clothes got out of the van. He spoke briefly with the two Latinos on the four-wheeler, then loaded the van himself. The four-wheeler drove away. Then the man made a phone call. A few minutes later an electrician's van pulled up and a Black guy wearing blue work clothes got out. The two men transferred the boxes from the Transit van to the electrician's van, then they both drove off.

"Think those are our guys?" Janet asked.

"Definitely worth a look," Allen replied.

They started after the vans, taking care to stay far behind. Both vans drove east on Interstate 8, then north on Arizona 85, headed for Phoenix. As they approached the city, traffic picked up, making it easier for Allen and Janet to tail them. The vans pulled into a Walmart Supercenter and parked at the far end of the parking lot. The Black guy got into the Transit van, and they drove away, leaving the electrician's van in the parking lot.

A few minutes later, a woman wearing jeans and a boatneck

sweater, her hair tied back in a ponytail, pulled up in an old Honda and drove away in the electrician's van. Allen and Janet followed. She drove the van into an industrial area—concrete block buildings with parking lots surrounded by concertina wire topped chain-link fences —and stopped at Gomez and Sons Auto Repairs, where she unlocked the gate in the chain-link fence.

Allen and Janet watched as she drove into the compound, pulled into a repair bay, and lowered the garage-style door. Then they parked at the curb with a good view of the gate and scooted down into their seats. About ten minutes later, she drove up to the gate on a motorcycle, relocked it, and took off down the road.

"Time to take a look," Allen said.

"Fingers crossed," Janet replied.

They crossed the street to the gate. Allen picked the lock on the gate, and they scurried up to the building, where they looked through a dirty window on the side of the auto repair shop. The lights were on in the repair bays, and they could see two vehicles—the electrical van and a white Suburban. They walked around the building to the front, looking in all the windows, but they didn't see any people or dogs. Janet banged on the window. No barking. Allen picked the lock on the front door, opened it, and turned to the burglar alarm keypad, the password breaker in his hand. "The alarm isn't armed."

"Seriously?"

"She must have been in too much of a hurry."

"If that's the only one," Janet said.

She opened the back door on the electrician's van. It was empty. Allen opened the liftback on the Suburban. The boxes from the four-wheeler were stacked inside. He tore the tape off the closest box and looked inside. Plastic bags full of pills.

He turned to Janet. "We're in business."

"Let's get out of here."

He opened the driver's side door. The key fob was lying in the seat. "Which one you want to drive?"

"I'll stick with the Frontier."

"You have the burner?"

She took a flip phone out of her pocket that had one phone number in the address book and laid it in the back of the electrician's van. "I'll open the bay door."

"Meet you at the Airbnb."

She pressed the button to open the garage-style door. Allen drove the Suburban out of the repair shop. Janet lowered the garage door, locked the front door behind her, and hustled out to the Nissan Frontier. They drove off in different directions, circling through the nearby neighborhoods until they were both sure that no one was following them, then each of them headed to the nearest on-ramp for Interstate 10.

The sun was coming up when they reached Tucson, where they stopped at an Airbnb on East Linden Street near the Tucson Botanical Gardens that they'd rented under an old alias. Their F-150 was parked on the street. Allen parked the Suburban in the garage. Janet parked the rental Nissan in the driveway and followed him inside.

"Now that we're in the clear, let's have a good look at what we've got," Janet said.

Allen pulled the untaped box to the back of the Suburban, lifted the flaps, and pulled out a gallon bag of pills in various colors. "Rainbow fentanyl."

Janet grabbed the side of the box and peered inside. "It's full. If all the other boxes are the same, this is millions of dollars retail. We don't want to be anywhere near this when the police arrive."

Allen nodded. "This is confiscate-the-house-and-put-everyone-in-prison drugs. Let's get out of here."

They left the Airbnb and drove back north, dropping off the rental truck before they returned to Gila Bend, where they drove through a Mexican restaurant for breakfast burritos and coffee.

AT 8:00 A.M., the manager arrived at Gomez and Sons Auto Repair and found the Suburban missing and the burner phone lying in the back of the electrician's van. He called Jasper Bell, the Black man who'd been driving the electrician's van, who rolled out of bed and drove over to the car repair shop to see for himself. Then Bell called Mr. Wishes.

"We've been hijacked."

"Explain."

Bell went through what happened, starting at the rest stop.

"So you changed cars, switched locations, Kitty drove the last leg, texted a photo of the Suburban, and locked up."

"Yes, sir."

"No one was tailing you?"

"We didn't see anyone."

"And there's a burner phone lying in the back of the electrician's van?"

"Yes, sir."

"I'll call back in a minute."

MR. WISHES WAS SITTING at a table in the back of the Bluebird Bar and Grill. Three men and one woman sat at the bar, nursing their morning drinks. The bartender glanced over at Mr. Wishes. He shook his head. It had been a long time since anyone really surprised him. Rip off the Orange Hill Cartel's drug shipment? It was a death sentence. No one with any sense would try it. The grifters had robbed his game and disrupted the El Paso gun and sex trafficking. Were they really stupid enough to hijack the cartel's fentanyl? Everything they'd done until they came after his card game indicated that they valued their lives. Otherwise, why did they run every time Sean and Phyllis caught up to them? What had changed? Why did they think that coming after the cartel was going to improve their situation?

He had a call to make. It wasn't going to be pleasant, but the longer he put it off, the worse it was going to be. He got out a different phone. "Mr. Elliot?"

"Mr. Wishes. Why are we speaking?"

"Our shipment has been hijacked."

"The one you guaranteed? Is this connected to your other problem, the one you put the contractors on?"

"It might be."

"You've always been reliable. A good earner. But anyone can over-stay their welcome if they can't deal with pest control. Do you understand?"

"Yes. I'll take care of it."

"In person. Not giving directions over the phone. I want you to be there on the ground making sure."

"I'm on my way." He ended the call, put away that phone, and called Sean on his usual burner.

"Have you found them yet?"

"No, sir. They're staying way under the radar. Our hacker set a program to churn through all the public surveillance cameras circling out from Albuquerque, but they haven't turned up anywhere yet."

"Someone just hijacked a shipment of ours. Looks like they plan to sell it back to us."

"Think it's them?"

"You know of anyone else that bold? Meet me in Tucson."

"We're on our way."

"Call when you're close by and I'll tell you where we're meeting."

Sean turned to Phyllis. "Did you hear all of that?"

She nodded. "You sure that lying to him was the way to go?"

"As opposed to telling him that you got shot and we got outma-neuvered? Yeah, I think it was the way to go."

"You think it was our targets that hijacked their shipment?"

"They were set up at the rest stop as if they were expecting some-thing to come through."

"If it's the grifters, they've got something else going on. This hijacking is too obvious. It points straight at them."

"I agree. Maybe we can raise the degree of difficulty."

He googled Freedom Bank and Trust and found the extension for Olivia Blevins. He called the number. It rolled over to voicemail. *"You have reached Olivia Blevins. I am not at my desk. Please leave a message and I'll get back to you."*

"A couple of players you're looking for are in Tucson." He ended the call.

"Think it will do any good?"

"Don't know. Had to try. But if it does, I'll probably end up owing you that steak dinner." He put his phone away. "Tomorrow, we drive down to Tucson. That's about the right amount of time if we drove over from Albuquerque. I'll call Terry and get him working on the public surveillance cameras down there. We'll see if we can find out more about the grifters' movements between Gila Bend and there. The next time we meet them, I want an ace up our sleeves."

MEANWHILE, Mr. Wishes called back Jasper Bell. "Open the burner phone."

"There's one number in the address book."

"Call it, put the burner on speaker, and leave this line open."

Bell did as he was told. The line rang three times before someone answered. "Who is this?" a man's voice asked.

"I'm the guy using the phone you left," Bell said.

"We've got your product. Must be worth millions of dollars. Do you want it back?"

"Yes."

"It'll cost you $300,000."

"It'll take a while to get that kind of money together."

"You have two days. Call me back when you have the money and we'll set up a trade." He ended the call.

Bell closed the burner phone and picked up the other phone. "Did you hear everything?"

"Yes," Mr. Wishes said.

"What do you want me to do?"

"Stand by. Make sure all our safe houses are secure. I'll bring the money."

"Yes, sir."

. . .

ALLEN AND JANET were back in their room at the Gila River Inn when they got the call from the burner phone they'd left in the electrician's van. After Allen ended the call, he turned to Janet. "We've got Mr. Wishes' attention. Now's where we find out if this plan has any legs."

Allen called Garcia on the same burner he'd used before, putting the call on speaker.

"Grifter," Garcia said, "I was beginning to wonder if you'd given up."

"I've got three big boxes of fentanyl pills—I'm guessing 120 pounds--that belong to the Orange Hill Cartel."

"Where are they?"

"Let's not get ahead of ourselves. Do you want to take down the Orange Hill Cartel or not?"

"Keep talking."

"We stole the pills. We're going to set up a meet where we sell them back. Your people stake out the pills, when Orange Hill comes to take them, you arrest them and roll up the crew."

"I can't guarantee that we'll be able to roll them all up. All I can guarantee is that we'll arrest whoever comes for the pills, and then we'll try to pressure them to provide evidence against their associates."

"Fair enough."

"Where are the pills? We have to make sure that we take them off the street."

"They're in the Tucson area. In a safe place. That's all I'm telling you for now. Get your people down to Tucson. When the Orange Hill Cartel is in play, I'll be in touch."

"I could just track this phone and arrest you."

"Go luck with that. You've got twenty-four hours to get your people down here."

"If Orange Hill gets away with the pills, it'll be on you."

"And how unusual it that?" Allen ended the call.

Janet squeezed his hand. "Good job, baby."

"What else was she going to say? Now we've got to see if she'll keep her word."

GARCIA CALLED AGENT SANDY LITTLE. "I just heard from the Travelers. Have you got them under surveillance?"

"We lost them for a few hours this morning."

"How did that happen?"

"They split up at a car repair place. Our guy went after the new vehicle, a white Suburban, but they lost him."

"One guy?"

"Trying to save money."

"The fentanyl is somewhere in Tucson."

"They haven't gone anywhere in Tucson since we got here."

"Except this morning."

"Won't happen again."

"Keep them close. If their plan goes south, we still want to be able to seize the drugs."

"We're on it."

OLIVIA BLEVINS CAME BACK to her office after lunch and checked her voicemail. Should she ignore the message? The thieves killed Barney and Robin without much effort. They weren't going to be able to capture them and make them give the money back. The money wasn't stolen from one of the bank's accounts, so there was nothing to cover up there. Still, it was a decision for Benny to make.

She walked across the hall. Jay wasn't at his desk, and Singh's office door was open. She knocked on the door as she entered. He glanced up from his laptop. "Just a second."

She closed the door and sat down in one of the chairs facing the desk.

"Okay," he said. "What's up?"

She told him about the voicemail.

He leaned back in his chair and stroked his chin. "The upside is obvious. Payback for the theft and for Barney and Robin. But what's the downside?"

"It's going to cost money," Olivia said. "There's no guarantee that we'll get them this time. And we don't know who left the message. It could be a setup."

"Yeah, it's either a setup or someone looking for help."

"If someone else is after the thieves, they might be easier to kill this time. But how did they know to contact us? Were they following the thieves from the beginning? Did they watch Barney and Robin walk into a trap? What will we be implicated in if we move forward?"

"FBI sting, you mean?"

"Whatever."

"I hear your concerns, but I would love to get even with the thieves if we can do it without substantial risk. Let's send a couple more of our security people just to look around. We need more information to make a firm decision."

"Okay. I'll take care of the details."

ALLEN AND JANET sat on the back patio of a barbeque restaurant that sat at a crossroads at the western edge of Gila Bend, ribs, coleslaw, and French fries in front of them. They had a clear view of their truck, where their gear bags and cash were stored. Allen carried his Glock under his shirt at his back. Janet's was in her shoulder bag. Allen's burner phone sat on the table beside him.

Allen shook the ice in his iced tea and set the glass on the table. "The day after tomorrow this will all be over with."

"Either for good or bad," Janet said.

"You think we're in over our heads?"

"No. Just don't want to jinx it. Should we switch motels?"

"If we stay where we are, someone might eventually find a public surveillance feed near the motel. But the more surveillance feeds we're on, the easier it will be to find us."

"An earlier feed won't lead them to us."

"No, but if they find us on any surveillance feed in this area, they'll focus their attention here, which increases the likelihood they'll find where we're staying before we're gone."

"How about if we switch hotels the night before we take the money? We'll only be there one day. It could add a fresh layer of chance."

"I like that. With any luck, Orange Hill will be too busy with the Feds to track us, at least for a few days. By then we'll be far ahead of them."

"When do we tell Garcia where the fentanyl is?"

"At the same time we tell Orange Hill, or maybe just before, which should increase the likelihood of all the them slamming straight into each other."

"It would be better if the Feds were waiting for them."

"Yes, it would, but we can't trust them to keep their end of the bargain. Even if Garcia wanted to, someone else might decide to go for the drugs ahead of time just to take credit."

"When do you think Sean and Phyllis will show up next?"

He shrugged. "Which one got shot? And how bad? Maybe they've left. Maybe they're stalking us right now. From here on out, anyone could be coming at us from any direction."

THE NEXT DAY, Mr. Wishes walked into the arrivals and departures lounge of Executive Air, a private airport located next to the Tucson International Airport. Jasper Bell and another man were waiting for him. He pointed to a baggage rack. "The three large bags are mine."

"Get the bags, Ramon," Bell said. He tuned to Mr. Wishes. "We're parked right out front."

He held the door for Mr. Wishes. The day was already hot, the bright sun casting a strong glare off the pavement. Mr. Wishes put on his sunglasses. "Anything happening?"

Bell shook his head. "Waiting for you."

Bell used the fob to unlock the white Ford Expedition and climbed into the front seat, where he started the SUV and turned up the air conditioning. Mr. Wishes got in the back seat and took out his burner phone. Ramon put the bags in the back of the SUV and got into the front passenger's seat.

Mr. Wishes called Sean, who answered on the third ring.

"Speaking."

"Have you found them yet?"

"Our hacker has set up a computer program to move through the surveillance footage of all the motels in the area. He'll start on restaurants next. It's just a matter of time."

"Meet us at the Rincon Mountain Visitors Center. We're in a white Expedition. What are you driving?"

"A gray Subaru Forester."

THE PARKING LOT was mostly empty at the Rincon Mountain Visitors Center. Bell parked the Expedition in the far corner of the lot with a clear path to the exit. They were there fifteen minutes before the Forester arrived and pulled up beside them. Sean and Phyllis got out, dressed like Baptist preachers.

"Stay in the car," Mr. Wishes said to Bell and Ramon.

He met Sean and Phyllis at the back of the SUV and raised the liftback. He pointed to a large gray duffel. "Here's some extra gear for you."

Sean slid the duffel out of the SUV and set it on the pavement. Mr. Wishes closed the liftback.

"Things may get a little tricky," he said. "You can't kill them until we know where our product is. So if you find them before you hear from me, stay on them and give me a call. If you know where they're staying, all the better, because the product might be there. Do we understand each other?"

"Completely."

"Good luck."

Sean picked up the duffel. "We're beyond luck. This time we're going to kill them for sure."

.   .   .

DIDO SAT AT HER WORKSTATION, the computer working through the public surveillance cameras in Tucson. It was slow and tedious business, particularly since there was nowhere to spiral out from to increase her chances of getting a hit. Her phone rang. It was Liz, one of their security people.

"Anything for us?" Liz asked.

"Not yet."

"Can't you hurry things up? Tommy has started flirting with the waitresses, and he's so bad at it, it's embarrassing to be sitting at the same table."

"Can't help you there. As soon as I have anything, I'll let you know."

Dido ended the call. They were definitely not the first team. She wondered if they would take the job more seriously if they knew what happened to Barney and Robin. Well, that decision was above her pay grade. Her orders were clear. Use Liz and Tommy for human intelligence and then report in.

14

Allen and Janet came out of the Gila River Inn carrying their gear bags. Their front left tire was flat. Allen shook his head. "What a pain in the ass."

He took the floormat out of the driver's side, set in on the pavement by the tire, and knelt down. He ran his hand over the tire, feeling along the surface, until he felt a hard edge. He turned on the flashlight on his smartphone and shined it in the wheel well, trying to light up the spot on the tire.

"We ran over a screw."

"Can we change it?"

"Look in the crew cab for the tools."

She searched the back seat. "No tools."

"We'll have to call someone."

She googled a tire repair place that did road service and gave them a call. A half hour later, a skinny, unshaven guy wearing greasy coveralls and his cap on backward pulled up beside them in a tow truck.

"You call about a flat?"

"Yeah," Allen said.

The man looked at the tire. "You got a spare?"

"In the bed of the truck."

The guy loosened the lug nuts, jacked up the front left side of the truck, removed the lug nuts, exchanged the wheels, and replaced the lug nuts. "There you go."

"Can the flat be repaired?" Janet asked.

"Looks like it could."

"Then take it with you and we'll follow you."

"We have to settle up first." The man wrote up a bill on his tablet computer and Allen paid using the Bixby credit card.

Allen and Janet got in their truck. "Probably got the flat in the gravel parking lot where we ate from that food truck," Allen said.

"The construction crew with the truckload of demolition debris?"

"Yeah."

"The trade-off of avoiding places with cameras."

TERRY CALLED SEAN. "I've found your grifters."

Sean put the phone on speaker. "Where?"

"Not in Tucson. Back up in Gila Bend at the Gila River Inn."

"What are they driving?"

"Silver Ford F-150 crew cab."

"You sure?"

"Let me text you a photo."

Sean and Phyllis looked at the photo in Sean's messages. The photo was at a strange angle in the distance, but it was the grifters. No doubt about it. "Why were you looking up there?" Phyllis asked.

"They were up there before, so I kept open a computer program checking interstate cameras. Figured that just because they were doing business in Tucson didn't mean they were staying there. Tagged them on an interstate camera a few days ago. My computer program hopscotched cameras to one at a convenience store across the street from the Gila River Inn today. Just pure luck that I found them."

"Are you sure they're still there?" Phyllis asked.

"Had them on the parking lot camera getting a flat tire changed thirty minutes ago."

"Great work, Terry" Sean said. "Hack into the motel's computer and find out their room number."

"Will do."

Sean texted Mr. Wishes. *Found them up in Gila Bend. On our way there now.*

Mr. Wishes replied, *Stay on them. Don't eliminate them until I give the go-ahead.*

Sean turned to Phyllis. "Map the quickest route up to Gila River Inn."

ALLEN AND JANET sat in the parking lot of Dusty's Discount Tires, waiting for their tire to be repaired. The tire store sat at an intersection across from a smoke shop and catercorner to a gas station. The manager came to the door and waved. A technician rolled the repaired tire over to their pickup truck and heaved it into the bed. Allen went into the office area, signed off on the work order and paid. When he got back to the truck, his burner phone rang.

"Hello?"

"We've got your money. Where do you want to meet?"

"This is how it works," Allen said. "You drop the money at a location we've chosen. After we collect it, we call with the location of the product."

"That doesn't work for us. How do we know you won't take our money and then sell the product to someone else?"

"'Cause that's not the way we work. And we don't want the product. We want the cash."

"I'm not convinced."

"You want your product? 'Cause this is the only way you're going to get it."

The line was quiet for a moment.

"You still there?" Allen asked.

"Yeah, I'm here. Where do you want to do the drop?"

"In Tucson, there's a park at East 22nd Street and South Country Club Road. At the playground next to the parking lot there's a trashcan at the end of a row of benches. Put the cash in that trashcan in a paper bag. The trashcan at the end of the row of benches. Do that at 8:00 a.m. tomorrow."

"When will you call back?"

"If it's not a trap and no one is watching for us, we'll call by 8:30."

"It won't be a trap."

"Great. You'll get your product and we'll get our money." Allen ended the call.

He turned to Janet and smiled. "Now we've got to get the pieces of the puzzle arranged. You better drive."

He called Garcia. "Did you get organized?"

"FBI and drug task force are in place in Tucson."

"You'll need to move fast. I'll be calling with the address of the stash house at about 8:15 a.m. tomorrow. Then I'll be calling the Orange Hill Cartel. So you ought to be able to get there in time to arrest them with the fentanyl."

"Why don't you just give me the location now? If we're set up ahead of time, you can be sure we'll catch all of them."

"The trust isn't there, Garcia."

"I've done what you've asked."

"You could still decide just to confiscate the drugs."

"What if we don't get there in time?"

"I'm confident you'll get there. You don't want those drugs on the street. Expect to hear from me at 8:15 a.m." He ended the call.

Janet smiled. "Looks like this plan is actually going to work."

"Which means it could go south at any moment."

"Spoilsport."

"I'd feel more comfortable if we knew where Sean and Phyllis were."

"I've got a feeling we're going to find out soon enough. Where do you want to eat?"

"Let's go to a steakhouse. Have a T-bone with sauteed mushrooms and a baked potato. Can you find one on your map app?"

"I'm on it."

SEAN AND PHYLLIS pulled into the parking lot of the Gila River Inn in Gila Bend and drove slowly through the parking lot. "Do you see their truck?"

"No."

Sean called Terry. "Do you know where the grifters are?"

"They were at a tire store on West Pima Street about forty minutes ago. Hold on a second." The line was quiet for a few minutes. "Their truck is parked outside Top Cut Steakhouse, a couple blocks farther into town."

"Did you find out their room number?"

"One-oh-five."

"Thanks." He ended the call and turned to Phyllis. "Let's have a quick look."

They parked in the lot across from room 105. A young couple came out of the room three doors down, chatting amicably, got into a Jeep Cherokee, and drove away. Sean and Phyllis got out of their Subaru Forester and went up to the door. He knocked. They couldn't hear any movement inside the room. Phyllis turned to watch the parking lot. Sean looked around the edges of the door and found a small piece of tape that had been set across the door to the frame to show if someone had opened the door. He removed it and stuck it to the door frame. Then he picked the lock.

Once inside, they moved quickly, checking the bathroom, the closet, and the drawers. No shower kits, no clothes in the closet or drawers. Two roller bags stood together next to the king-size bed. Phyllis turned to Sean. "Not planning to stay, are they?"

They laid the roller bags on the bed and opened them. Just clothes and shower kits.

"These bags could belong to anyone," Sean said.

"They must carry everything with them."

"Wouldn't you?"

They put the roller bags back as they found them, locked the door to the room, and replaced the tape. After they got back to their SUV, Sean noticed he had a text message on his phone from Mr. Wishes.

"What is it?" Phyllis asked.

"Money drop around 8:00 a.m. So we need to be stalking them by seven or so."

"Full gear?"

He nodded. "We're not taking any chances."

"Look," Phyllis said. "Here they come."

Sean and Phyllis ducked down in their seats and waited while Allen and Janet parked in front of their room.

"Close call," Phyllis said.

"We're inside their bubble again."

"Should we put a tracker on the truck?"

"Good idea."

After Allen and Janet entered the room, Sean slipped out of their Forester, snuck up behind the Ford F-150, and placed the tracker. Then he hurried back to the SUV.

"Tracker works," Phyllis said.

"Great." Sean started the SUV. "Let's hide around the corner until we're sure they're in for the night."

ALLEN AND JANET stood in the middle of their motel room. "I've got the feeling that someone's been in here," Janet asked.

"Nothing's been moved."

"I know."

"Too many footprints in the carpeting to see if anyone's been here." Allen looked in the bathroom and opened the closet. "Better look in our bags."

They lifted their bags onto the bed and opened them. "My bag is just as I packed it," Janet said.

"Mine too," Allen replied. He went to the window and peered outside. No one was in the parking lot. He turned to Janet. "We're doing the deed tomorrow. We were talking about changing motels today. Let's do it. We could move to a motel in Tucson. Cut down on our timeline in the morning."

"You really want to do this?"

"Yep."

They rolled their bags out to the F-150 and put them in the back seat on top of their gear bags. Then they pulled out of the parking lot, Allen driving.

"Thanks for humoring me," she said.

"Didn't want to hear the 'I told you so' if we got ambushed here in the morning."

SEAN AND PHYLLIS WAITED, Phyllis watching the tracker app, until the F-150 was three blocks away, then they followed.

"Glad we didn't leave already," Phyllis said. "We're going to be able to kill them at will. Catch them in the open and shoot them down before they have a chance to react."

"As soon as we have the go-ahead from Mr. Wishes."

"Everything they've got is in that truck, so if they're carrying any cash, we're going to be able to take it."

"And their gear." Sean smiled. "It's about time things went our way."

"We deserve it," Phyllis replied. "This job has dragged on way too long."

"That's the truth."

ALLEN AND JANET checked into the downtown Tucson Red Roof Inn and carried their bags upstairs to room 224.

"Nicer than some we've been in on the run," Janet said.

"Two miles from the I-10 in a business district where we won't stand out. Besides, it's just one night."

"Should we bring our gear up?"

"I don't want to, but I think we should. We'd be in a hell of a jam if someone stole the truck with our Kevlar and weapons in it."

. . .

SEAN AND PHYLLIS, parked in the corner of the Red Roof Inn parking lot, watched Allen and Janet pull their gear bags out of the F-150 and lug them across the lot to the motel.

"So this is where they're staying for the night," Phyllis said.

"All tucked in. Find the nearest motel."

She googled nearby motels on her phone. "There's a Comfort Inn just up the interstate."

"The drop is at 8:00 a.m. If we're up at 6:30 a.m., we should be in good shape."

"Tail them from here?"

"That would be best. But with the tracker, we can always find them at the drop site."

AGENT SANDY LITTLE CALLED GARCIA. "Someone's following the Travelers."

"Any indication who they're working for?"

"None. They look like professionals. Not law enforcement."

"Don't let them interfere with the Travelers until we have the fentanyl."

"How far can we go?"

"All the way. We can't let the fentanyl slip through our hands."

A HALF HOUR LATER, Allen came out of the motel and went to the F-150 in the parking lot. He glanced around nonchalantly. No one in a parked car. No one walking through the parking lot. He slid under the bed of the truck and spotted the tracker, its red on-light pulsing. He slid out from under the truck and sauntered back into the motel.

When he got back to their second-floor room, Janet turned from the window.

"Anyone?" he asked.

She shook her head. "No one was watching you."

"Well, you were right. Someone's onto us. There's a tracker on the truck."

"Did you leave it there?"

"Yeah. Let them think we don't know."

"Think it's Sean and Phyllis?"

"I hope so. Don't need any new players in this game."

DIDO LOOKED at the image on her computer screen of Allen and Janet crossing the parking lot of the Red Roof Inn. She pushed back from her desk and called Liz. "Found them."

"Where?"

"Red Roof Inn in downtown Tucson."

"How?"

"Pure dumb luck."

"The boss still wants them taken care of?"

"The boss wants you to assess the situation and decide if you can deal with them without incident. Do not try to take them in their motel room. If you believe it's doable, pick a spot in the open where you have room to maneuver. Do you understand?"

"Loud and clear."

15

The next morning, at 7:30 a.m., Allen and Janet drove by the playground at Reid Park. There was no one in the playground. An older woman wearing hiking clothes walked a Scottie on a nearby path. Allen made a U-turn, drove back, and parked in the parking lot facing the exit. They slid down in their seats and waited. No one pulled into the parking lot or walked into the playground from the walking path.

Allen looked at his watch. 8:00 a.m. "Ready?"

Janet nodded. She climbed out of the truck, strolled by the benches, reached into the trashcan, and took out a paper grocery bag. She looked inside. Bundles of one-hundred-dollar bills. She strolled back to the truck. As soon as she closed the door, Allen put the truck in gear. He drove down East 22nd Street, headed for the I-10.

Janet pulled a money bundle at random and thumbed through it, then she counted the bundles. "$300,000 is all here."

"Is it real?"

She took an ultraviolet pen from the glovebox and pulled three one-hundred-dollar bills at random. When she shined the ultraviolet light on each bill, the security ribbon to the left of Ben Franklin's portrait glowed pink. "Yeah, it's real. Now we just have to hold onto it."

Allen pulled over into a 7-Eleven convenience store and drove around the side of the building. He called Garcia. "The fentanyl is in an Airbnb on East Linden Street." He gave her the street address. "It's in a Suburban in the garage. You get a fifteen-minute head start." He ended the call.

Janet said, "I'm going to scout the area and get something to drink. Want anything?"

"No. I'll wait here."

Three cars were at the gas pumps. She went inside, used the restroom, and stood in line to pay for her coffee drink. Just the usual headed-to-work crowd. No one remotely suspicious.

Allen looked at her quizzically when she got in the truck. "All clear," she said.

"The fifteen minutes are up." He called the Orange Hill number and gave them the same information that he had given Garcia. Then he pulled back onto East 22nd Street.

"We need to switch vehicles," Janet said.

"And lose the tracker? No way. Mr. Wishes is done. Now it's time to deal with Sean and Phyllis. Get them off us for good."

"How do you want to handle it?"

"Let's get away from Tucson. Take them on a wild goose chase to build up their confidence."

Janet looked at the map app on her phone. "How about the I-10 east to Las Cruces, New Mexico?"

"Works for me."

The traffic was light as they approached the I-10 interchange. "Someone's behind us," Allen said. "A gray Nissan Rogue. White people. Not Sean and Phyllis."

Janet looked over her shoulder. "Test them."

Allen got onto the on-ramp. The Rogue followed. He got off at the first exit, took a right, and turned into a Chevron gas station. The Rogue drove by. He pulled out of the Chevron station and drove back toward the interstate. The Rogue was behind them.

"You were right," Janet said.

"Of course I was right," Allen replied. "Those idiots couldn't tail a blind man."

"Think they're Orange Hill?"

"No way. Not the Feds either."

"Singh's?"

"I have no idea."

He drove past the on-ramp, under the overpass, and continued on 29th Street, then he sped up, took a right turn into the neighborhood and made a series of left and right turns, driving as fast as he could and ignoring the stop signs.

"Lost them," Janet said.

He got back on I-10. "Now we see if Sean and Phyllis come after us."

Mr. Wishes, Bell, and Ramon drove slowing by the Airbnb on East Linden Street. Everything was quiet. A few vehicles were parked on the street, but there were no work trucks or suspicious SUVs. They circled the block and pulled up into the driveway. Bell walked up to the front door and rang the doorbell. No answer. He picked the door lock and went inside. Sofas, chairs, big TV, nothing out of the ordinary. He walked through the kitchen and out into the two-car garage. A white Suburban was parked inside. He pressed the garage door opener on the wall by the door to the kitchen. The door went up.

Mr. Wishes and Ramon got out of the Ford Expedition and came into the garage. Ramon raised the liftback on the Suburban and opened the flaps on the nearest cardboard box. Mr. Wishes looked inside. Bags of rainbow fentanyl.

He called Sean. "Are you still tracking the grifters?"

"Yes."

"Deal with them and bring me the money."

He turned to Ramon and Bell. "Put the boxes in the back of the Expedition."

As Ramon and Bell were carrying the boxes back to the SUV,

three black Ford Explorers squealed up into the driveway, blocking them in, and FBI SWAT members in tactical gear came running around the sides of the house. Mr. Wishes backed away from Ramon and Bell and raised his hands.

"Federal Agents! On the ground now!"

Mr. Wishes, Ramon, and Bell lay down on the driveway. SWAT members cuffed their hands behind their backs and took possession of the boxes. The FBI special agent leading the SWAT team called Garcia. "Got the fentanyl and three men. Two of them appear to be blue collar, but the third looks like management."

"Great work."

"Thanks for your help."

"My pleasure. Hope the interrogations lead somewhere."

The special agent ended the call.

GARCIA CALLED Agent Little on her office land line. "Have you still got the Travelers under surveillance?"

"Yeah, they're very popular. Two crews are tailing them now."

"We've got the fentanyl."

"Congratulations, boss. Do you want us to arrest the Travelers?"

"No. Let them go."

"What about the crews that are chasing them?"

"Not our problem. If the Travelers outrun the people who are after them, they might be useful in the future."

"What about the ransom money?"

"The Orange Hill money? I hope it disappears. I don't want to be at a Senate Oversight committee hearing explaining how we used criminals to break a drug-smuggling ring."

"Roger that."

"Be on the first flight home."

TOMMY PULLED over on the side of the street in a no parking zone, and Liz called Dido. "They spotted us and ditched us. Can you find them?"

"Where did they spot you?"

"On the I-10 heading east."

"Where did they lose you?"

"In a neighborhood near 29th Street."

"Where do you think they went?"

"Best guess? Back on the I-10."

"East or west?"

"Don't know."

"Get near the freeway and wait for my call."

Dido opened a computer program to start searching through the security cameras at the freeway on-ramps and welcome centers. The trail couldn't be any colder, but maybe she'd get lucky again. At least it was billable hours.

MEANWHILE, Sean and Phyllis, wearing Kevlar vests, their gear bag in the front seat, had been following the Rogue, watching the F-150 outmaneuver them. When it was clear that the F-150 had lost the Rogue, they followed the tracker down I-10 east, increasing their speed as they left Tucson and the traffic began to thin out.

"Must have been Singh's people," Sean said.

"This crew is even worse than the last. Only reason they're not dead is they couldn't catch up to the grifters," Phyllis replied.

As they passed the sign for the University of Arizona Tech Park, they saw the Ford F-150 in the distance passing a semitruck. "Hand me a Glock," Sean said.

Phyllis reached into their gear bag and handed him the pistol. He slipped it into the water bottle holder in his door. Then Phyllis pulled out an AR-15 rifle, unfolded the stock, and shoved a full magazine into place.

He stepped on the accelerator and the Forester shot forward, passing a pickup truck and a Toyota Corolla. As they started around the semi-truck, the F-150 picked up speed.

"They know we're on them," Phyllis said.

"Take out their tires."

Phyllis unhooked her seat belt, lowered her window, and hung out of the door to fire her rifle. Bullets peppered the back of the truck, which started swerving between lanes.

As Allen veered right, a bullet shattered the passenger's side outside mirror on the F-150. "That's definitely Sean and Phyllis," Janet said. "They must have been following the tracker."

"Brace yourself," Allen said, "I'm taking the exit."

They barreled down the ramp. Allen stomped on the brakes. The truck fishtailed and he worked the steering wheel to keep from spinning. He glanced both ways and ran the stop sign at the end of the ramp, taking a right and accelerating down the highway.

"County fairgrounds to the right," Janet said.

"Okay. It's as good a spot as any."

They turned right onto the access road to the fairgrounds and rolled along on the dusty gravel. Up ahead was a small concrete block building in front of a chain-link fence. The gate was locked. Allen slid to a stop at the side of the building. "Assuming the Feds got Mr. Wishes, Sean and Phyllis don't have backup. Our best chance is to fight them here. Use the building for cover."

They jumped out of the truck. Allen dragged their gear bags from the back seat and pulled on his Kevlar vest before he grabbed an AR-15 and three magazines and ran out a hundred feet from the building and lay down in the road. The gravel dust was blowing away. He could see the gray Subaru Forester coming.

Janet slipped on her vest, lugged the gear bags into the front seat, and squeezed the truck around the back of the building. Then she got out and lay down next to the right side of the building.

The Subaru came at them fast, throwing up a cloud of dust, but Allen waited until the first bullet struck the road near him before he opened fire, flattening both front tires. The Subaru careened sideways and screeched to a halt.

. . .

SEAN AND PHYLLIS climbed out on the passenger's side. "This is a killing field," Sean said. "We don't want to be here too long."

He peeked around the bumper of the Subaru. A bullet smashed into the fender over his head. "Good thing he's not much of a shot."

They sat in the road with their backs against the flat tire.

"We can't rush them," Phyllis said.

"No, we can't. We need backup." Sean got out his burner phone and speed-dialed Mr. Wishes.

"Hello?" a voice said.

"Who is this?" Sean asked.

"Who is this? You called this phone."

Sean ended the call. He turned to Phyllis. "Something's wrong. I'm guessing Mr. Wishes has been compromised."

"So there's nothing for us here?"

"At this point, if we manage to kill them, I don't know if we'll get paid."

"We'll get the cash they're carrying."

"Orange Hill will want their money back."

"We can't just drive away from here," Phyllis said. "We've got two flat tires."

"We could run off to the right and keep going, stay off the road until we're sure they're gone."

"How about if we try talking? We've got nothing to lose," she said.

"Hey," Sean hollered.

"Hey," Allen replied.

"No reason to continue with this."

"Why's that?"

"Seems Mr. Wishes is out of the picture."

"That was the plan."

"We're not employees. We're contractors. We don't work if we're not going to get paid."

"That puts you in a bad place."

"We're going to walk off into the field on your left. You can drive away."

"Leave your guns."

"Can't do that. You might be vindictive."

"Then I guess we all take our chances."

ALLEN JUMPED up and ran back to the building. "What do you think?" he asked Janet. "Kill or no kill."

"Hey," Janet called from the corner of the building. "Is the contract off?"

"Yes," Sean replied. "You won't see us again. Can't speak for anyone else."

Janet turned to Allen. "I'd love to kill them for the trouble they've caused us, but it was always just business for them. Let's give them a chance."

Allen yelled, "Go on out into the field."

Allen and Janet watched Sean and Phyllis walk away from the Subaru, their rifles down at their sides.

"Let's go," Allen said.

They climbed back into the truck. Allen eased out from behind the building, turned back onto the gravel road the way they had come, and stomped on the gas. Gravel flew as they sped around the Subaru, Janet keeping her rifle trained on Sean and Phyllis.

"Close call," Janet said.

"Is there any other kind?"

They turned left onto the highway heading back toward the interstate. When the on-ramp was in sight, Allen pulled over on the shoulder. "Time to get rid of the tracker."

A school bus drove by, heading in the direction of the fairground. He went to the back of the truck, looked under the bed, found the tracker, and pulled it. Then he held it up for Janet to see before he threw it into the field. A Toyota Tundra flew by. He trotted back to the driver's door and climbed into the truck.

"When do you think they placed the tracker?" Janet asked.

Allen shook his head. "Sometime after we got to Tucson. But precisely? Who knows?"

"So they waited to come after us?"

"Mr. Wishes needed his product."

"Do you think we're really done with him?"

"We've done everything we can to make his life hard and disrupt the cartel's plans."

Allen watched for a break in traffic and pulled out onto the highway. "We need a new ride. This one is full of bullet holes. Call Billy. See if he knows a helpful used car dealer in this area."

SEAN AND PHYLLIS stood in the weedy field and watched the grifters drive away. "Good riddance," Phyllis said.

"We've got to wipe down that car and the gear. Dust ourselves off. Walk to somewhere we can call a ride," Sean said.

"Keep the Glocks?"

"Yeah."

Two hours later they were on the north side of the interstate near a subdivision. Phyllis took out her phone to call an Uber. "Back to the motel?"

Sean nodded. "Pack and take the shuttle to the airport."

Once they were in their motel room, Phyllis sat on the bed and kicked off her shoes. "I'm going to shower and change clothes."

Sean took out his laptop computer and googled for news reports involving drug busts. He found a video of Mr. Wishes and two others being perp-walked into the Phoenix federal courthouse.

"Come look at this."

Phyllis looked at the screen over his shoulder. "Well, that's all done."

"We wasted a lot of time."

"And money. You think the Orange Hill Cartel will reimburse us?"

"I think they'll kill anyone they think is involved in this mess. Get us airplane tickets to anywhere that's not here," Sean said.

"Do Mr. Wishes' bosses know we were involved?"

"I don't know. He's the only one we ever worked with. I imagine his bosses know about the grifters, but us? If we're lucky, he was keeping us to himself so that he could take the credit for eliminating the grifters."

"They certainly were a challenge."

"They're definitely top competitors. Get the tickets, then take a shower."

OLIVIA BLEVINS WAS in a meeting listening to a presentation when her burner phone buzzed in her pocket. She made a show of looking at her watch and then left the room. She walked down the hall to an empty office, shut the door, and locked it. The phone was still buzzing. Dido.

"Yes?"

"It's a no-go here. Our team lost the target. There's been a major drug bust. The police are buzzing around, hoping to scoop up some more players."

"You don't know where the targets have gone?"

"They're in the wind."

"Thanks for the effort."

"You bet."

16

Allen and Janet stood in the manager's office of Straight Arrow Used Cars. The manager, a middle-age woman with a smoker's mouth and a washed-out perm, stood on the other side of the desk.

"I'm not going to ask you any questions," she said. "Billy vouched for you. That's good enough for me."

"So can you help us?" Allen asked.

"I've got a low mileage Cadillac Escalade, four-wheel-drive. Clean as a whistle. Clear title."

"You'll take the truck and make it disappear? Chop shop or car crusher?"

"Absolutely. How do you want to handle the registration?"

"Tom Bixby." He took out the Tom Bixby driver's license and passed it to her. "What's this service going to cost?"

"Seventy thousand in cash. That's the vehicle plus the extras."

He glanced at Janet. She opened her canvas tote, pulled out a banded bundle of one-hundred-dollar bills, and counted out $70,000 onto the desk. The manager pulled a bill at random and looked at it with an ultraviolet light pen. The embedded thread glowed pink.

"No offense," she said.

"None taken," he replied.

"I imagine you'll want to pass a police road stop."

"Of course."

She scooped the $70,000 into her desk drawer. "Have a seat while I get the paperwork ready. It'll just take a few minutes."

Allen and Janet sat in the chairs facing the desk. Allen eased the Glock out of his coat pocket and laid it in his lap. Janet put her right hand into her tote.

"Bad feeling?" Janet whispered.

"No, it's just the point where we have the least control."

Ten minutes later, the manager came back into the room. Allen slipped the Glock into his coat pocket. "Bill of sale and title transfer." She pointed to signature lines on both documents. "Sign here and here."

Allen signed.

"I've put a license plate on the Escalade. I'll transfer it to you. Do you have an Arizona address you want to use?"

"No."

"I'll take care of it."

"Is that everything?"

"The SUV is around back, next to the truck."

The Escalade and the F-150 sat side-by-side by the air conditioner compressor. Allen scanned the car lot. No one was in this part of the lot. He and Janet transferred their gear and their bags to the Escalade.

"Good luck," the manager said.

"You bet," Allen replied.

Allen drove out onto the highway, heading for the interstate.

Janet got out her phone. "We still heading for Las Cruces?

"It's as good a destination as any."

After they took the ramp onto the interstate, Allen got out his Garcia burner phone and put it on speaker.

"I was wondering when I'd hear from you," she said.

"Did you get the Orange Hill people and the drugs?"

"Yes."

"What did I tell you?"

"Why are we talking?"

"Could you do me a tiny favor?"

"No. You didn't do this to be a good citizen. You did it to help yourself."

"But I still helped you."

"Answer is *no*." She ended the call.

Allen changed to the left lane, lowered the window and threw the phone out. It shattered on the shoulder, the pieces bouncing into the grass median.

"Exactly what I expected," Janet said.

"Had to try," Allen replied. He passed a Greyhound bus and moved into the right lane. "How did we end up doing?"

"We made about $500,000 overall, but we have to pay Billy."

"So what do you guess we made after expenses?"

"Around $275,000 or $300,000? Something like that—between our cash and the bank account," she said.

"That's plenty to run on. Let's stay off the radar for another six months."

"Dump the credit cards?"

"Definitely. Anyone tracing the Bixby cards could find us within a few days. Better throw them away."

"What about staying with Tomas on the Navajo reservation? There's no surveillance for miles."

"Great idea. Tomas will put us up, no question, especially if we give him a gratuity. He's on the reservation north of Gallup, isn't he?

"Yes. On the New Mexico side."

"Have we got a good phone number for him?"

"I'm pretty sure he's in the encrypted address book in our cloud account."

"Send him a text and then plot a course north from Las Cruces."

A MONTH LATER, Missy Drake was back at Freedom Bank and Trust in Rocky Shore, Missouri, sitting in Benny Singh's office with Singh and Olivia.

"How are you?" Olivia asked.

"I'm fine."

"And your mother?"

"She's well. Thanks for asking."

"Edibles working for her?" Singh asked.

Missy nodded. "Yes."

"That's great. How do our trust accounts look?"

"Everything is as it should be."

"That's great to hear."

"I've been thinking," Missy said.

"About what?" Olivia asked.

"I'm taking a lot of risk. I think I should be paid something for my trouble."

"Like what?"

"Like whatever Carl was being paid."

"There're a lot of people with their hands out," Singh said. "The money only goes so far."

"Well, it seems to me that I'm a key player. Maybe someone less important should take a pay cut. How's Carl adding value now?"

Olivia nodded. "I understand what you're saying. How about if we pay you a thousand a month right now and then go up to two thousand after we make some changes?"

"How long to make the changes?"

"A few months."

"Okay. I'm willing to be a team player. But in two months, I'm expecting to receive my due."

"Thanks for being so understanding. How do you want to receive your money?"

"Cash."

Singh went into his desk drawer and took out an accordion envelope. He counted out ten one-hundred-dollar bills and pushed them across the desk toward Missy.

She picked them up and folded them into her pocket. "See you next month."

Missy went out into the bank's parking lot, got into her car, and drove to a nearby parking deck next to a shopping mall, where FBI Special Agent Lannister was waiting for her in a black Ford Explorer.

"Could you hear everything?" Missy asked.

"Yes," Lannister said. "We've got their admissions. And you've got their money."

Missy pulled the wad of one-hundred-dollar bills from her pocket. Special Agent Lannister put it into an envelope, wrote the amount on the outside, sealed it, and signed his name across the sealed flap.

"How much longer do I have to do this?"

"We've got them, but we want to get anyone else they're involved with. Based on this recording, we're going to get wire taps onto Carl Thompson's, Olivia Blevins's, and Benny Singh's phones. Within a month, we should have everything we need for the grand jury."

"And me?"

"The drug transportation charge is going to disappear, and you'll get a commendation in your work record."

"Thank you."

"Just what you deserve. I wish more citizens took their responsibilities as seriously as you do. Sorry we can't help with your mother."

"I'm moving her to a care facility in Illinois. Farther to drive to see her, but the edibles won't be a problem anymore."

A WEEK LATER, midmorning, while Singh was working at his desk, he got a text from Thompson on his burner phone. *Meet me in the parking lot of Soldiers Memorial Park.*

Singh deleted the message. What could this be about? He drove out to the park, which was located north of downtown. At this time of the day, there were only four cars in the parking lot and two moms with their toddlers in the playground. He spotted Carl sitting on a park bench near a walking path. He got out of his car and joined him.

"What's up?"

Thompson glanced around. "You weren't followed, were you?"

"I don't think so."

"You don't think so, or you know so?"

"I wasn't followed. What's all this about?"

"Something's up."

"What do you mean?"

"A work friend told me that I'm being investigated."

Singh sighed. "By who and for what?"

"That's not clear. Nothing good. Could just be a normal review. Could be someone complained about my evaluation of their bank."

"But you don't think so."

"No, I don't. They moved me away from your bank, and now they're looking into me. Hold on to my money until you hear from me again. Just in case."

"Okay."

"And watch yourself. Don't do anything that might draw attention."

IN VANCOUVER, Canada, the contract killers Sean and Phyllis came back to their hotel suite to pack their bags. The man they'd been sent to kill was lying naked in a dumpster behind a Chinese restaurant.

"All jobs should be that easy," Phyllis said.

"Hardest part was heaving his fat ass into the dumpster," Sean replied.

"He didn't even beg. Knew we had him dead to rights, knew it was time to stop running."

Sean used the keycard to open the hotel room door. Inside, two men, one white and one Asian, were lounging on the sofa, pistols in their hands. Sean reached into his coat and Phyllis stepped away to his right.

"Let's not get hasty," the Asian said. "If we wanted to kill you, we wouldn't be sitting on your couch."

"What do you want?"

"You took a job from the Orange Hill Cartel."

"We took a job from Mr. Wishes," Phyllis said.

"Same thing," the Asian said.

"Keep talking," Sean said.

"Do you plan on finishing the job?"

"Don't know where the grifters are."

"They're on the Navajo reservation in northwest New Mexico."

"That's a big place, mostly without cell service or internet access. Almost impossible to track anyone there."

"They're staying with Tomas Nez. He runs a chop shop in the desert south of Shiprock."

"If you know where they are, why don't you take care of them?"

"Because that would make things more complicated than they need to be," the white man said. "We've got other business on the rez."

"If you want us to help you, it's going to cost you. Those two grifters are harder to kill than cockroaches," Sean said.

"You're not backing out on our deal. You agreed to do the job, so now you're going to finish it."

The Asian continued. "But we do realize this job is more difficult that anyone could have foreseen, so we'll double your fee."

"Double?" Phyllis said. "We spent more than that already."

The Asian shrugged. "Not our problem."

"We'll need proof of death," the white man said. "That's close-up photos of severed hands with the fingerprints intact or severed heads with the faces intact."

"Okay," Sean said. "We'll get it done."

"We're expecting to hear good things."

THREE DAYS LATER, while working at his desk at the bank, Singh got another text from Thompson. *Dump this phone.* What the hell? Had Carl gone off the rails or were they really in deep trouble?

He pulled the SIM card, snapped it in two, and stomped on the phone until the screen was broken. Then he walked down the hall to the men's room, tossed the phone into a sink, and filled the sink with water. After it soaked for a few minutes, he pulled it from the sink and tossed it in the trash. It was definitely a paperweight now. What next? Should he run? Or was Carl being investigated for a reason entirely unconnected to Freedom Bank and Trust?

When Singh got back to his office, he sat down at his desk and started doodling on a notepad. If Carl was right, and he waited too long, he'd be arrested. He'd go to jail for sure. But if Carl was wrong, and he ran, he'd never be able to come back to this life. He'd be an international fugitive. He'd never see his kids again. At least, not on a daily or weekly basis. Maybe once or twice a year.

Giving up this life wouldn't be so much of a hardship, not if he had enough money. But he didn't want to out himself as an embezzler if he didn't have to. Missy Drake had asked for money two weeks ago. A week later, Carl told him he was being investigated. Now Carl told him to destroy the phone. He must be worried that he's about to be arrested.

Singh opened his laptop computer, put in his password, and looked over the amounts in the trust accounts. If he took a third from each account and moved it to his Geneva account, he'd be set for life, and the account holders would still have plenty of money. They'd be angry, of course, probably sue the bank, but he'd be long gone.

He set a program to move the money from the trust accounts overnight. Then he went into his travel app and booked a flight to London at 4:30 this afternoon. From there, he'd be able to catch a train for France and disappear.

AT 6:30 P.M., Singh got off his flight to O'Hare International Airport in Chicago and walked over to the departures screen. His flight to London was still on time at 9:00 p.m. He walked down the concourse through the sea of travelers pulling roller bags, taking the moving sidewalk whenever possible. When he got near his departure gate, he found a sports bar and got a table in the back.

While he was waiting for his server, two men in suits approached his table. "Mr. Singh? Mr. Benjamin Singh?" the closest man said.

"Yes?"

The man showed his identification. "FBI. We need for you to come with us."

"What's this about?"

"We'll discuss that at our offices."

"Am I under arrest?"

"Do you want to make a scene, or can we read you your rights in the car?"

Singh stood up.

"Give me your passport."

He dug his passport out of his jacket pocket and handed it over.

"Let's go."

BACK IN ROCKY SHORE, Missouri, Olivia Blevins sat in an interview room at the Sheriff's Department. FBI Special Agent Lannister sat across the table from her.

"Carl Thompson has already given you up, Ms. Blevins."

"I don't know what you're talking about."

"Thompson says that you approached him to overlook your embezzlement in exchange for a monthly payment."

"Not true."

"That's what he says." Lannister's phone rang. He glanced at the number and took the call. "Yeah?" He listened. "Okay. Good work."

"Your partner, Benny Singh, was just apprehended at O'Hare International Airport. He was on his way to the UK."

"That's not possible. It doesn't make sense."

"It makes perfect sense. He took the money and left you to take the fall."

"I've got nothing to do with any embezzlement."

"Just keep saying that. Thompson took a deal. Either you or Singh is going to take the final deal. Whoever's left is taking the fall. Is it going to be you or Singh? He doesn't care about you. Do yourself a favor."

"I want to see a lawyer."

"Suit yourself."

17

The contract killers Sean and Phyllis, dressed in jeans and canvas jackets, sat in a white Suburban in the MacDonald's parking lot across the street from a Marathon gas station in Shiprock, New Mexico.

"White folks and Indians," Phyllis said, "we stand out here worse than we do in small town Tennessee."

"Tomas Nez comes by here almost every day, so it's still our best shot," Sean replied.

"We need a better surveillance spot if we're going to pretend to be photographers."

A Navajo police cruiser pulled up beside them and a patrol officer got out. Sean lowered his window. "Yes, sir?"

"License and registration."

"On what basis? We're parked."

"You are not a member of the nation. We can ask for your ID whenever we want."

"My license is in my wallet in my back pocket. The registration is in the glove box."

The officer nodded.

Sean took out his wallet and handed the officer a Colorado

driver's license in the name of John Hawkes. "Could you get the registration, honey?"

Phyllis took the matching car registration from the glove box. The officer examined them both.

"What brings you here?"

"Photography—we're traveling all over the four corners region taking pictures for a coffee table book."

"Can I see your commercial photography permit?"

Sean took the permit out of the inside pocket on his jacket and handed it over.

"Sit tight."

The officer went back to his cruiser. Sean sat with his hands on the steering wheel. A few minutes later, the officer returned and handed back the driver's license, car registration, and photography permit. "How long are you planning to be in the area?"

"Probably going to take a few weeks to take all the pictures we need, and we'll be traveling all over the reservation."

"Is that right?"

"It's a beautiful place."

"Take care."

The officer got back in his cruiser and drove away.

Phyllis put the registration back in the glove box. "Should we move to another spot?"

"That would seem suspicious." He put his driver's license back into his wallet. "Do you want some coffee?"

"That would be great."

Sean went into the MacDonald's, bought two coffees, and came back out to the Suburban. He handed one of the coffees to Phyllis.

"Thanks," she said. She took off the lid. "How long should we stay here?"

He glanced at his watch. "A little while longer. If he doesn't come by here by 10:00 a.m., he's not coming."

They sipped their coffee and watched the road. At 9:55, a black Honda Ridgeline drove by.

"That was him," Phyllis said.

Sean pulled out of the MacDonald's parking lot and followed the Ridgeline down highway 491 south past the Shiprock airstrip. The highway was deserted. Sean drove well back, and Phyllis watched the pickup truck through binoculars.

About thirty minutes outside of town, the pickup turned right onto a dirt road and Nez got out and opened a ranch gate. Then the pickup continued down the road. Sean pulled over at the gate. He and Phyllis got out, went around to the back of the Suburban, raised the liftback, and unboxed a drone. Sean set the drone on the ground a few feet from the SUV, and Phyllis used the controller to launch it. Then she guided it down the road until she could see the Ridgeline on the screen and followed it to a compound surrounded by a barbwire fence. A long, sheet-metal building took up a quarter of the space. Behind it was a smaller, faded-red barn with missing shingles. The rest of the property was filled by rows of junk cars. Three pickup trucks were parked in front of the sheet-metal building.

She hovered the drone over the compound, watching as Nez got out of his truck and went into the building.

"Looks like an auto salvage operation," she said.

"Must be the cover for Nez's chop shop," Sean said.

"Wish we could see inside the building."

"Intel places them here," Sean replied. "Either they're here or the intel is shit. Keep watch while I work our alibi."

Sean got out a digital camera and walked away from the Suburban, taking pictures of the surrounding desert and the mountains at the horizon.

An old pickup driven by an Indian wearing a feed store cap crept by. Sean smiled and waved. A few minutes later, another police cruiser drove by. Phyllis waved. Sean acted as if he was concentrating on taking a photo. When Phyllis turned back to the controller, she saw a man walk from the warehouse to the barn. She zoomed in with the drone camera and took his picture.

"Sean, I think I've got something."

Sean trotted back to the SUV. He looked at the photo. "It's overhead, but that is definitely the male grifter."

"Want to wait to see if we get a picture of the female?"

"No need."

Phyllis guided the drone back to their location and landed it by the Suburban. Sean put it in the back of the SUV, and they drove back toward town.

"Looks pretty deserted out at the chop shop," Phyllis said

"It does. But maybe it gets busy at night."

"Should we come back and do another reconnoiter?"

"That would be best. We don't want to make another mistake. Let's come back late, like 2:00 or 2:30 a.m. Send the drone up. If it's all quiet, we could go in then."

"What about the cops?"

"It's worth the risk," Sean replied. "The cops usually run a skeleton crew that late. Probably be one officer by himself."

"We can claim to be taking night pictures to complement the day pictures."

"And if he challenges us, we can shoot him and leave him in the ditch. No one will notice until daylight at least."

"We're still going to need a lot of luck if we're going to kill the grifters."

"We can do this."

"I know."

"We're the best," Sean said. "We're going to win. Their luck is going to run out and our skill is going to carry us."

"You're right."

"Of course I'm right. We don't need to re-analyze how they managed to escape before. They're not going to get away this time."

BACK AT THE COMPOUND, Allen, Janet, and Tomas Nez sat around a card table in the sheet-metal building drinking coffee. Two men in stained coveralls were pulling the engine from a Ram truck, while another man was removing the passenger's side door from a Prius that had been T-boned on the driver's side.

"Are you sure the drone saw you?" Nez asked.

"The way I was ambling along, I don't see how they could have missed me," Allen replied.

"Awfully quiet. Not much louder than the wind in the trees."

"Technology. Makes our work harder and easier."

"And you're sure it was looking for you, not checking out my operation?"

"One hundred percent? Nothing's one hundred percent. But we've explained our situation."

"It's surprising that they caught up with us," Janet said. "But Orange Hill has business all along the border. It could be as simple as word innocently leaking out from here."

"Anyway," Allen said, "if it's Orange Hill, I expect them to come in hot in the next few days."

Nez nodded. "Let me assemble some guys. We'll dig a trench out back. Anyone shows, we'll bushwhack them and put them in the ground. Then you can get out of here."

"Thanks for the offer," Allen said. "But we don't want witnesses, not even if you vouch for them. Besides, if Orange Hill smells a trap, they'll just wait. We'd rather deal with them now."

"Suit yourself."

"Just leave the digger with the keys in it," Janet said. "We'll cut a trench if we need it."

"And if you've got any body armor," Allen added, "we could use one more set."

THAT EVENING, after Nez and his employees left, Allen and Janet sat at Nez's desk watching the surveillance cameras that were positioned at the front gate and the corners of the sheet-metal building. An owl flitted overhead, three coyotes crept past the fence, and a small wolf stopped at the front gate and looked up at the camera as if she knew what it was.

"You can sleep," Allen said.

"I can't sleep," Janet replied. "Too worked up."

"I think this is finally it," he said.

"Why?"

"I've just got a feeling."

"Poking the bear might not have been the best idea."

"Well, on the upside, we've got a pile of money."

"And we might be dead by morning."

He took her hand. "I love you."

"Did you think way back then when you spotted me walking along the side of the road that we'd be together this long?"

"Didn't really have the ability to think along those lines. But here we are. Still alive and still free."

She picked up his hand and kissed it. "Us against the world."

"Always."

"How many do you think are coming?"

"Don't know. Don't care. Going to kill them all."

"Do you think it will be Sean and Phyllis?"

"That would be very stupid on their part. We already gave them a pass."

"Maybe they don't have a choice."

"There's always a choice. They could choose running."

"Professional killers don't run," Janet said.

"True. They're not really cut out for it."

"So, no hesitation."

"Absolutely none."

They heard a whirring over the monitor.

"That must be the drone. Time to get into position," Allen said.

Janet stood up, tugged her Kevlar vest down, and checked her assault rifle to make sure it was on auto-fire.

"You good?" Allen asked.

"Ready or not, here I come."

OUTSIDE THE CHAIN-LINK FENCE, Sean and Phyllis were lying on the sand, scanning around the building with their night-vision goggles.

"See anyone?" Phyllis asked.

"No."

"Think they've left?"

"They're probably inside."

"I don't like it."

"Me, either."

"Set it on fire and see who comes out?"

"You can see a fire out here for miles," Sean said. "Police and fire department could get here before we have a chance to get away."

"So we're busting in?"

"Yeah. Windows have bars. You take the back door and I'll take the front."

"Okay."

"Turn on your comms set."

They both turned on their communications headsets and clicked off the safeties on their AR-15 rifles.

They ran at a crouch to the front gate. Sean pulled a pair of bolt cutters from his backpack and cut the chain to the padlock. He scurried toward the front, where he crouched to the left side of the door. Phyllis rushed down the side of the building, glancing at the windows for any light that might indicate where the grifters were, turned the corner, and got down on one knee by the back door.

Phyllis tapped her comms. "In position."

"Go," Sean replied.

Sean kicked in the front door, firing his rifle as he burst into the building, and rolled to the left toward the garage door. He stopped firing and crawled under a pickup truck just as Phyllis rushed in the back, fired a burst, and pivoted into the open door of a bedroom. Empty. She ran down the hall, fired another burst, and dove behind a tool cabinet in the chop shop. The room was quiet.

Phyllis looked to the right of the cabinet. A long worktable, covered in tools and auto parts, ran down the wall. She shifted to the left of the cabinet. A refrigerator and a section of kitchen cabinet sat against the wall. Two folding tables surrounded by folding chairs sat in the open area that led to a small office. The door hung open. She could see the dull glow of a computer screen. Directly in front of her was a pickup truck sitting on blocks, its engine hanging on chains from a pulley system. Where were the grifters? She tapped her comms. "Nothing."

"Ditto," came the reply. "Create a diversion."

She sprang to her feet and shot a burst through the windshield of the closest truck, avoiding the engine. The shot smashed through the windshield, back glass, and the windshield of the second truck. She dropped to the floor.

While she was firing, Sean squirmed out from under his truck and sprang toward the office. As she dropped to the floor, he sprayed the office with gunfire and rolled through the doorway.

"Anything?" Phyllis whispered.

"Nothing," Sean replied.

JANET, balancing herself on the truck frame inside the empty engine compartment, turned her face to keep the windshield glass from falling into her eyes. Allen was on their comms. "One of them's in the office."

She quietly lowered herself to the floor. With the truck on blocks, she was completely exposed. She rolled onto her belly and fired a short burst under the tool cabinet. Someone, a woman, moaned. It must have been Phyllis.

"Stay on her," Allen said.

Allen rose up in the bed of the second truck and lowered himself over the side. He couldn't move fast. He was wearing the full body armor he bought in Phoenix. He'd been hit twice, both times in the chest, but he was unharmed. He clicked his rifle to full auto, and moved toward the office, firing through the wall as he came. Sean sprang out of the office and fired a burst that banged off Allen's chest plate.

Allen shot Sean in the legs. Sean lurched sideways and collapsed to the floor. Allen kicked his rifle away. Then he spoke into his comms. "Take her."

Janet scrambled out from under the truck, rushed to the tool cabinet, and pushed it out of the way. Phyllis lay in a tangle, blood leaking from her neck. Janet snatched her rifle out of her hands and tossed it away. The she grabbed her by her Kevlar vest and dragged her over to Allen and Sean.

"I knew you were the best," Allen said.

Janet smiled. "Flattery will get you everywhere."

Allen looked at Sean. "Can you see her?"

"Yes."

"Neither one of you is going to live, but you could suffer for a long time."

Sean sucked in a breath. "What do you want?"

"Orange Hill send you?"

He nodded. "After the last throwdown, we didn't want to come, but we didn't want them after us."

"They can be persuasive."

Janet cut in. "So they didn't trust you?"

"No."

"Wanted proof?"

"Close-up photos of amputated hands, or photos of decapitated heads."

"Well," Allen continued, "I'm sorry things turned out this way."

"No, you're not," Sean replied.

"You're right. I'm not. You should have tried harder not to come after us." He turned to Janet. "Can you get his phone, baby? Too hard to squat in this rig."

She patted Sean down and found his phone in his pants pocket.

"Unlock it," Allen said.

She held it to Sean's face, then handed it to Allen, who scrolled through the address book. "This Orange Hill's number?"

Janet showed the phone number to Sean.

"Yes."

"Let's get this over with," Sean said. "Do her first, so I know she's not suffering."

Allen nodded to Janet. She shot Phyllis in the face.

"Satisfied?"

Sean nodded. "She was a good partner."

Janet unhooked the Velcro on Sean's Kevlar vest, pushed the end of her rifle under it, and fired two shots into his chest. He shuddered and was gone.

She turned to Allen. "Just in case we need to open his phone again."

Allen and Janet took off their body armor and stacked it near the door where two tarps were lying. Then they laid out the tarps, rolled Sean and Phyllis up in them, carried them out back one by one, and laid them down behind the old barn where Nez had left the digger.

Allen climbed up on the machine and dug a trench ten feet long and six feet deep.

Janet was waiting by the rolled-up tarps. "What are we going to do about the Orange Hill Cartel? They're just going to send someone else."

"I know." He looked off to the east. "It won't be dark much longer. Let's finish this up."

They carried the tarps to the trench and tossed them in. Then Allen got back in the digger to fill the trench. He dropped the blade to push the earth into the trench and then turned off the machine.

"What's up?" Janet asked.

"What if in the course of killing us, we got badly burned? They wouldn't have been able to provide the evidence that the cartel wants. All they could do would be to show two burned up bodies. Think it could work?"

"Maybe. But the skin would have to be completely burned, or they'd know the bodies were Black."

"Best idea I could come up with."

"It might work."

Allen found a gas can in the barn. They climbed down into the trench, unrolled the bodies, and lay them face up. Allen used Sean's face to open his phone, then he poured gasoline over the bodies and set them on fire. An hour and a half later, the bodies were unrecognizable, just human figures wearing Kevlar. Allen used Sean's phone to take a photo of the burned remains and then texted it to the Orange Hill Cartel.

They got burned in the firefight. This is all there is. They're as dead as they could be.

The reply came: *We'll send your money the usual way.*

"Wonder how long that will hold up?" Janet asked.

"I guess we'll find out." Allen tossed Sean's phone down beside his body, climbed up into the digger, and pushed the earth into the trench. When he was done, he rolled the digger over the filled trench to compact the dirt. The he put the digger back where Nez had left it.

"I hope we never come up against anyone better than them," Phyllis said.

"They were real professionals, but they still made mistakes."

"Thank God."

"Let's wash up," Allen said.

They went into the room they'd been staying in at the back of the chop shop, stripped off their filthy clothes, and got in the shower together. They kissed and held each other for a minute as the water sluiced down their bodies. "Wish we had time to celebrate," Janet said.

"Me too," Allen replied. "But we need to get out of here."

They had just finished dressing and organizing their gear when Nez arrived at 7:00 a.m.

"Smells like burned meat," he said.

"It will blow off by noon. Have you got a new ride for us? Something that will stand up to a police stop or a roadblock?"

"You leaving the Cadillac Escalade?"

"Orange Hill found us. We know you didn't turn on us, so the cartel must have found out about the car."

"I've got a Dodge truck I came by legit. Owner passed away. His son sold it to me. Still registered and tagged."

"Sounds good."

"Let me pull it around for you."

Nez walked out into the yard.

"You think the car dealer sold us out?" Janet asked.

"I don't know. I'm just not taking any chances."

Nez parked the truck in front of the chop shop, and Allen and Janet loaded their gear into the back seat.

"Where are you headed?" Nez asked.

"Don't know yet," Allen said.

"Thanks for your help," Janet added.

"You got a job going where you need me, get in touch."

"You bet."

Allen and Janet drove away.

MR. WISHES SAT with his back against the wall in the day room of the Maricopa County Fourth Avenue Jail. He had been denied bail and was awaiting trial on drug smuggling charges. Two dangerous looking men sat with him, facial tattoos and badly-stitched scars, one on his left and one on his right. It had taken him two months to consolidate his authority over the white gang and reach an accommodation with the Black gang and the Latino gang, even with the help of the Orange Hill Cartel applying pressure on the outside. No one in the jail was happy about this situation except for him, but he was left with no choice when the various gangs wouldn't leave him alone.

A bald Black man with a white beard, sitting across the room, gave him a meaningful glance. Drug buyer. He tapped the man sitting to his right, and he whispered to the tattooed man sitting beside him. This man walked off and the Black man followed him.

Bell and Ramon had both taken deals and been transferred to facilities in Colorado and Georgia. Bell had been murdered in his cell, and Ramon was in solitary confinement for his own protection. Who knew how long that would last? Bell's testimony implicated Mr. Wishes and Ramon's testimony supported Bell's, so the case against Mr. Wishes was much weaker than it had been originally.

A guard came up to him, standing on the opposite side of the table. "You've got a phone call."

Mr. Wishes got up, followed by his bodyguards, and followed the guard down the hallway to a wall phone by the guard's station. He answered the phone. "Yes?"

"The grifters you were looking for? You can stop looking."

"Thanks."

"You bet."

He hung up the phone. The grifters were dead. It was a shame it took so long to kill them. If Sean and Phyllis had finished them off before they stole the fentanyl, he wouldn't be sitting here and he wouldn't be in the doghouse with the cartel.

"Good news?" the bodyguard on his left asked.

"Yeah. A little late, but good news."

They walked back to the day room. The tattooed man was already back at their table. The cartel was cleaning up loose ends. If they managed to get to Ramon, he was the only one left. He had to make sure that no one could kill him, not the other gangs and not the Orange Hill Cartel. Once he was out of jail, he'd be able to prove his loyalty, and life would go back to normal. Meanwhile, he was on his own. He needed to keep selling drugs in the jail so that he could pay for his protection. But he also needed to make sure he didn't get caught. Adding to his charges while he was in jail was the worst thing he could do.

TWO WEEKS LATER, Allen stood at the table in the privacy room next to the safety deposit vault of Unity Bank in Montgomery, Alabama. He opened the tray, took out the drivers' licenses and credit cards for Maureen and Gray Abernathy, put the cards in his front pocket and closed the tray. The teller was waiting in the hall. She took the tray, locked it back into its spot, and brought him the key.

"Thanks," he said.

He looked out the front door. A slow drizzle had started. He jogged across the parking lot and climbed in the passenger's side of a Cadillac.

"Find everything?" Janet asked.

"Got the IDs and credit cards."

"So now we start our new life."

"Looks that way."

"When we get back to the hotel, I'll move the money from the Portland bank to the Montgomery bank. Then we'll be ready to go on vacation."

"Still planning on saving for the future?" Allen asked.

"I don't want to, but we need to. Let's say we save half the money. Put it in the Cayman account we've been using as a laundry."

"How much money are we talking about?"

Janet took out her smartphone, opened the calculator app, and started inputting numbers. "After expenses, we still have about $250,000."

"Let's keep $100,000 and put away the rest."

"So we're on vacation for six months."

"Sounds about right. We should start putting out feelers for a new job—we want to be picky—and we should buy two new identities."

"What about if we start our vacation by going on a cruise down the Mississippi River, just to make sure no one is after us?"

"Sounds like a plan."

"I love you."

"I love you."

Janet backed out of their parking space. "Honey, in the future, how about if we avoid working any of the big cartels?"

"That's a good idea, and certainly safer, but sometimes we've just got to follow the money."

She sighed. "I thought you were going to say that."

"What? We're alive, aren't we? Free and living our lives. You know you like a good adrenaline rush."

"Yeah, but there're close calls and close calls. I prefer the first over the second."

"Just trying to show you a good time, baby."

"Where do you want to stop for the night?"

"Where do we catch the cruise ship?"

"Minneapolis."

"Are there still reservations available?"

"There were when I checked yesterday."

"Yesterday? How long have you been thinking about making this trip?"

"Just looking and dreaming."

"Let's see if we can make it to Memphis today."

FINALLY

Thanks for reading *The Contract Killers*. If you enjoyed it, please post a short review on a review site of your choice. A few words will do. Honest reviews are the number one way I attract new readers. Thanks so much.

I'd love to hear from you. You can reach me at my website: https://michaelpking.org

ALSO BY MICHAEL P KING